Fever/Dream

an adaptation of Calderón's
Life is a Dream

by Sheila Callaghan

A SAMUEL FRENCH ACTING EDITION

SAMUEL
FRENCH
FOUNDED 1830
NEW YORK HOLLYWOOD LONDON TORONTO
SAMUELFRENCH.COM

ISBN 978-0-573-69924-5   Printed in U.S.A.   #29868

MUSIC USE NOTE

Licensees are solely responsible for obtaining formal written permission from copyright owners to use copyrighted music in the performance of this play and are strongly cautioned to do so. If no such permission is obtained by the licensee, then the licensee must use only original music that the licensee owns and controls. Licensees are solely responsible and liable for all music clearances and shall indemnify the copyright owners of the play and their licensing agent, Samuel French, Inc., against any costs, expenses, losses and liabilities arising from the use of music by licensees.

IMPORTANT BILLING AND CREDIT
REQUIREMENTS

All producers of *FEVER/DREAM must* give credit to the Author of the Play in all programs distributed in connection with performances of the Play, and in all instances in which the title of the Play appears for the purposes of advertising, publicizing or otherwise exploiting the Play and/or a production. The name of the Author *must* appear on a separate line on which no other name appears, immediately following the title and must appear in size of type not less than fifty percent of the size of the title type.

In addition the following credit *must* be given in all programs and publicity information distributed in association with this piece:

Originally produced June 2009 by
Woolly Mammoth Theatre Company, Washington, DC,
Howard Shalwitz, Artistic Director;
Jeffrey Herrmann, Managing Director.

FEVER/DREAM was commissioned by the Occidental College Theater Department, where it received a workshop production in the fall of 2007 in collaboration with Jessica Kubzansky. The production was directed by Jessica Kubzansky, with set design by Susan Gratch, costume design by Tom Slotten, lighting by Rachel Levy, composition/sound by Bruno Louchouarn, choreography by John Pennington, and projections by Kari Swanson. The cast was as follows:

CLAIRE	Lizzie Adelman
ROSE	Reba Buhr
SEGIS	Grayson DeJesus
ASTON MARTIN	Lucky Gretzinger
STELLA STRONG	Anna Gibson
FRED CLOTALDO	Alex Marshall
BILL BASIL	Dan Selon
CHORUS (ACCOUNTANTS,	
ASSOCIATES, & SECURITY GUARDS)	Richie DeMaria, Maura FitzGerald, Eli Isaacs, Doug Locke, Daniele Manzin, Kaja Martin, Jonny Rodgers, Joanna Schubert, Jonathan Stoner, Dana Vigran

FEVER/DREAM was originally produced in June 2009 by Woolly Mammoth Theatre Company, Washington, DC (Howard Shalwitz, Artistic Director; Jeffrey Herrmann, Managing Director). The production was directed by Howard Shalwitz, with set design by Misha Kachman, costume design by Franklin Labovitz, lighting by Colin K. Bills, sound by Veronika Vorel, choreography by Meisha Bosma, video design by Evan Martella, and properties by Jennifer Sheetz. The cast was as follows:

CLAIRE	Jessica Frances Dukes
SEGIS	Daniel Eichner
BILL BASIL	Drew Eshelman
ROSE	Kimberly Gilbert
STELLA STRONG	Kate Eastwood Norris
ASTON MARTIN	Kenyatta Rogers
FRED CLOTALDO	Michael Willis
CHORUS (ACCOUNTANTS,	
ASSOCIATES, & SECURITY GUARDS)	Andrew Blau, Lauren Ciandella, Michael Davis, Alice Gibson, Mark Halpern, Shannon Listol, Amanda Miller, Katie Rooney, Matt Sparacino, Anastasia Stewart, Scott Whalen

CHARACTERS

SEGIS

ROSE

CLAIRE

FRED CLOTALDO

SECURITY GUARDS

STELLA STRONG

ASTON MARTIN

BILL BASIL

ACCOUNTANTS

4 ASSOCIATES

AUTHOR'S NOTES

A stroke (/) marks the point of interruption in overlapping dialogue. When the stroke is not immediately followed by text, the next line should occur on the last syllable of the word before the slash – not an overlap but a concise interruption.

Special thanks to Jill Soloway, Leah Hamos, Bryan Joseph Lee, Miriam Weisfeld, Alana Dietz, Elissa Goetschius, the Occidental College Theatre Department, the staff of New Dramatists, Sally Ollove, Quincy Long, Dana Eskelson, Gus Schulenburg, and Flux Theatre.

ACT ONE

(The basement. Darkness.)

(Sounds: dripping water. Rumbling boiler. A fluorescent light struggling to buzz on, no light. An ancient fax machine. Maybe the room is lit [very vaguely] by the little green "ON" switches on all the old machines.)

(We're here for quite a while, taking in the sounds.)

(Then:)

(The sound of an old-fashioned office phone ring.)

(Once.)

(Twice.)

(A voice in the darkness, the voice of **SEGIS***:)*

SEGIS. CustomerservicehowmayIhelpyou.

(The light flickers on for a tiny moment. We see the hunched figure of a man over a desk piled with papers.)

(Darkness again. Silence. Then:)

I'msosorrytohearyou'vebeenhavingtroubles.

(The light buzzes on again, this time for longer.)

(We see: puddles of water on the floor near tangled electrical equipment. Exposed pipes. Piles and piles of papers. A drain in the center of the floor. An ancient fax machine. Grey concrete. Beat-up metal filing cabinets. Towering messy piles of papers. An enormous sign that reads "NO TRESPASSING.")

(Also, stacks and stacks of books. Text books, reference books, literature, etc.)

(It's a graveyard for outdated equipment.)

(Yellowing newspaper clippings are pasted to the wall and the floor, along with several yellowing newspaper photos of **BILL BASIL**. *The articles are highlighted and circled here and there.)*

(Centrally: A rusted freight elevator door from the 40's, with old numbers up to 77 and a wand.)

(A chute off to the side.)

(We can smell the asbestos.)

(SEGIS *wears a T-shirt, stained and foul, and a pair of horrendous jeans. He is unshaven, unwashed, and grips the phone receiver as though it's part of his hand. His beard is down to his chest and his hair hangs in greasy ropes down his back.)*

SEGIS. *(cont.)* Thismustbeveryfrustratingforyou.

(A pile of papers drops from the chute. Seconds later, an apple. Then, a handful of loose cooked macaroni and some lettuce leaves.)

(The fluorescent light buzzes off again. Darkness.)

I'llconnectyouwithbillingimmediately,thankyouforcalling.

(Silence, save the ubiquitous ambient noise.)

(More silence.)

(The phone rings again.)

CustomerservicehowmayIhelpyou.

(a beat)

I'llconnectyouwithbillingimmediately,thankyouforcalling.

(Suddenly, a sound we haven't heard before…a screeching of metallic, then a booming sonorous 'waaannnnnnng," then the sound of un-oiled gears turning.)

(The entire room shakes.)

(In the darkness, a dirty yellow light flickers behind the panel of the freight elevator. The wand moves very very slowly from the letter L to the letter B.)

(The noise stops.)

(Then, the miserable creak of a stuck metal door trying to slide open.)

(Inside the lit elevator, two figures. One is dressed as a bike messenger, complete with helmet and shoulder bag. The other is a nerdy little thing.)

(They are both frozen in terror.)

ROSE. Where the heck are we?

CLAIRE. Um.

ROSE. What button did you push?

CLAIRE. I didn't. Your bag must have –

ROSE. WOW WOW WOW. WHAT IS THAT SMELL.

CLAIRE. Rosie –

ROSE. Don't call me that.

CLAIRE. Something died here…something large….

ROSE. Where's the light?

*(**ROSE** fumbles around for a light switch.)*

CLAIRE. …when a thing decomposes the particles are released into the air so the smell is actually tiny little pieces of dead-thing….

ROSE. Claire, I wanna – okay this might not be the time for this conversation…

CLAIRE. I know what you're / going to say

ROSE. But you promised you would hold / it together

CLAIRE. Right, right…

ROSE. You have a Very Important Role in all this

CLAIRE. I know, / I know

ROSE. And I REALLY like, need you to…Oh, wait, huh…

CLAIRE. What?

ROSE. Feels like a, a breaker, or…

*(**ROSE** flips a switch. Worklight floods the room. **SEGIS** stares at them in terror. They stare back. No one moves.)*

CLAIRE. *(horrified whisper)* WHAT IS THAT?

ROSE. *(quietly)* Don't…

CLAIRE. WHAT IS THAT?

ROSE. …move…

> (**SEGIS** *moves slightly. The girls yelp and run to the other side of the room.*)

SEGIS. Customerservicehowmay Ihelpyou.

ROSE. Oh hi. We're looking for the 77th floor…

SEGIS. I'msosorrytohearyou'vebeenhavingtroubles.

CLAIRE. He's nice! He's nice!

ROSE. Thanks. I think we're okay now. Looks like you were just about to have lunch…sorry to bother you….

SEGIS. Thismustbeveryfrustratingforyou!!

ROSE. Um, yeah…

> (**SEGIS** *lunges at the two. The girls scream.*)

> (*We see his ankle is chained to his desk. The chair upon which he sits is stuck to his body, as is the phone receiver.*)

SEGIS. I'llconnectyouwithbillingimmediately,thankyouforc alling!!!

> (*He lunges again. The girls are less fearful.*)

THANK YOU FOR CALLING HAVE A NICE DAY!!!!

ROSE. You're hurting yourself.

SEGIS. THANK YOU FOR THANK YOU FOR HAVE A NICE CONNECT YOU WITH SORRY FOR YOUR INCONVENIENCE INCONVENIENCE PISSING INTO A DRAIN ON THE FLOOR MACARONI'S ARE ALREADY COLD STAPLER STOPPED WORKING THREE HUNDRED AND THIRTEEN MONTHS AGO WHAT IS THAT SOUND?

> (*He stops a minute. Listens.*)

What is that sound?

> (*Again.*)

It's me. Talking. To someone else. This is what I sound like talking to someone else. I have language again. I'm looking at you. You're brighter. You are brighter and you have two eyes. I'm looking at them, they are looking back. Say something.

ROSE. I wish I wasn't here.

SEGIS. Ha! Trailing from your lips, the words in little spirals, "wish"…"wasn't"…wip wip wip…Do it again…

ROSE. I wish you weren't here.

SEGIS. Wip wip wip…

(He unpries his fingers from the phone receiver, one by one, screaming in pain. Then he flexes his hand with much difficulty.)

ROSE. How long have you been here?

SEGIS. Long time.

ROSE. Who put you down here?

SEGIS. I'm not a prisoner.

ROSE. So this is a choice?

SEGIS. It's a JOB.

ROSE. Do I look like a moron Claire?

CLAIRE. Normally no, but in that outfit –

ROSE. People don't get stuck in the basements of corporate buildings for nothing. And I'm guessing you didn't chain yourself to that desk…

SEGIS. Things could be worse. Things could break. My machines, for example. I didn't always have to push staples through stacks of paper with my thumb.

*(**ROSE** begins cracking up.)*

ROSE. What kind of idiot is chained to a desk pissing into a drain and thinks it's part of his JOB?

*(Abruptly, **SEGIS** hurls his broken stapler across the room. It smashes against the wall, leaving a dent.)*

(The women jump a little.)

SEGIS. Every moment you remain unharmed in my presence is a moment I am giving you. *That's* a choice.

ROSE. Wow. You are INTIMIDATING.

CLAIRE. Rose.

ROSE. No really. I am INTIMIDATED right now. Aren't you INTIMIDATED, Claire?

CLAIRE. Yes! Fire exit! Where?

(**CLAIRE** *searches desperately for a fire exit.*)

(*Suddenly,* **SEGIS** *grabs a pair of dull scissors from his desk and slams them into the lock on his chain. The lock breaks.*)

(*He then pries his body from his chair with a roar. As he stands, slowly and painfully, every vertebra in his back cracks one by one.*)

(*Standing at full height, he is menacing. He drags his chain closer to the women, gripping his dull scissors.*)

(**CLAIRE** *cringes.* **ROSE** *steels herself.*)

(*Much to the women's surprise,* **SEGIS** *lays back on his desk, motionless for several moments.*)

(**CLAIRE** *ferrets out their escape, while* **ROSE** *studies* **SEGIS** *carefully.*)

(*After a long pause…*)

SEGIS. Do you have a cigarette?

ROSE. *(a lie)* I haven't smoked since I was seventeen…

(**SEGIS** *snifs the air near* **ROSE**'s *bag.*)

SEGIS. Check your bag.

(**ROSE** *checks her bag. She pulls out a pack of Lucky Strikes as* **CLAIRE** *inspects the room.*)

ROSE. Hey! Look at that. Claire?

CLAIRE. *(waving it away)* I'm getting my share of pollution from the asbestos, thanks. Ho, a dot matrix!

(**ROSE** *hands a cigarette to* **SEGIS**. *He sits up [with diffi- culty, he's still cramped] and places the cigarette between the fingers of his claw hand. She lights it. He inhales it reverently. He coughs.*)

SEGIS. *(re: the cigarette)* I've only ever read about these… What's on your head?

ROSE. I'm a bike messenger.

SEGIS. What's that?

ROSE. I ride around on a bike delivering packages.

SEGIS. I thought MY job sucked.

CLAIRE. A mimeograph…mama…

SEGIS. What are you delivering today?

ROSE. Nothing. My honor. Whatever. It's none of your business.

(CLAIRE begins reading the newspaper clippings on the walls and floor.)

SEGIS. Careful with those…

CLAIRE. "April 22, 1984…After Fierce Dispute, Erratic Corporate Tycoon Bill Basil Clinches Five Billion Dollar Takeover"…"June 5, 1998…

SEGIS. "Basil Bulldozes Competition Once Again"…

(CLAIRE holds up another clipping. SEGIS recites it from memory.)

"January 7, 2002…What Makes Bill Basil Tick?"

CLAIRE. You're good.

ROSE. What are those?

SEGIS. Blueprints.

ROSE. For what?

SEGIS. For becoming the most powerful man in the world.

ROSE. A goal of yours?

SEGIS. A dream, one might say.

ROSE. I don't see much opportunity for growth in your department…

SEGIS. Isn't that the point of dreaming? To visualize the fantastic, the implausible?

(Abruptly and viciously, SEGIS sits up and begins to beat the ancient fax machine with the arm of a broken swivel chair. He works into quite a frenzy.)

(ROSE and CLAIRE are startled.)

(Finally, he stops. He's in a lot of pain from the exertion.)

SEGIS. *(cont.)* They have detectors for the smoke. They're coming.

ROSE. Who?

CLAIRE. Rose…

(**CLAIRE** *points to the freight elevator. The wand is slowly climbing down from the 77th floor.*)

(**SEGIS** *moves to a stack of papers and begins chewing holes into the corners.*)

ROSE. Who? Who is coming??

CLAIRE. *(panicked)* Is there another way out? Trapped, are we trapped?

SEGIS. Ms. Nicotine, Ms. Asbestos, thankyousomuchforyourcall, weappreciateyourbusiness.

ROSE. Stop that!

SEGIS. Weappreciateyourbusiness, pleasecallagain.

CLAIRE. No windows! Can't breathe!

ROSE. Tell us what's going on.

SEGIS. Pleasecallagain haveaniceday.

(*Shriek of gears, etc. The freight elevator door opens.* **FRED CLOTALDO** *emerges with two* **SECURITY GUARDS**. **FRED** *immediately gags from the smell.*)

FRED CLOTALDO. A wall of stench…No smoking, okay. Is that so diffic –

(*He spots* **ROSE** *and* **CLAIRE**.)

Who…

ROSE. I'm a messenger. Look.

(*She shows him her bag.*)

FRED CLOTALDO. This is not a public, the lobby is the –

| **ROSE.** I hit the wrong button. | **CLAIRE.** She hit the wrong button. |

ROSE. I was trying to get to the 77th floor. I have a package.

FRED CLOTALDO. Who's it for?

(**ROSE** *digs into her bag and pulls out a padded mailer. She reads the name.*)

ROSE. A mister "Aston Martin."

(*He holds out his hand to take the package.* **ROSE** *doesn't move.*)

It says "deliver in person."

FRED CLOTALDO. Give it to me.

ROSE. *(re:* **SEGIS***)* What's he doing down here? Why was he chained to the desk?

(**FRED CLOTALDO** *turns to his* **SECURITY GUARDS***.*)

FRED CLOTALDO. What happens when you go out for a moccachino? Hm? Exhibit A. So, thank you. Thank you for this headache. Arrest them.

(*The* **SECURITY GUARDS** *arrest* **ROSE** *and* **CLAIRE***.*)

ROSE. This is SO illegal, okay.

(**FRED CLOTALDO** *casually gestures to the NO TRESPASSING sign.*)

FRED CLOTALDO. I'm assuming you can read.

ROSE. It was an ACCIDENT.

SEGIS. Let them go, Fred.

FRED CLOTALDO. Oh look, you have language again. First time you've said something real to me in months. Anything more to add?

(**SEGIS** *says nothing.*)

Well that's fine. Month after month I come down to this stinkhole with books, magazines, articles…I GAVE you that language, mister.

(*He finds* **SEGIS***'s cigarette.*)

A WHOLE CIGARETTE? You are just SOPPING in treasures right now, aren't you? I don't suppose you'll need that new Swingline any more…

(**SEGIS** *looks desperate.*)

SEGIS. I –

FRED CLOTALDO. Hm?

SEGIS. Thankyousomuchforyour business, we'llbehappytoa cceptanymajorcreditcards.

FRED CLOTALDO. Thought so.

(**FRED CLOTALDO** *kicks at the lock to* **SEGIS**'s *chain.*)

Put that back on.

(*Obediently,* **SEGIS** *returns the lock to his ankle.*)

Thank you.

(**SEGIS** *nods and continues biting holes in the corners of papers.* **FRED** *hands him some books.*)

Brought you some more reading. *Plato's Republic. Identity and Rhetoric. The Times, the Post, the Weekly,* and a 'zine. Enjoy.

(*beat*)

You're a good kid. Sorry I yelled, son.

SEGIS. I'm not your son. I don't have a father.

(**FRED CLOTALDO** *freezes a moment, hurt, but decides to say nothing. He hits a button to call the freight elevator.*)

(*to the guards*) Take them to central booking. I have a meeting.

CLAIRE. That's the clink. Is that the clink?

ROSE. But my package….

CLAIRE. I've never been to the clink before.

ROSE. It's urgent. He…Mr. Martin…

FRED CLOTALDO. I'll see that he gets it.

CLAIRE. CLINK! The sound the door makes when you lock it.

(**FRED CLOTALDO** *holds out his hand for the package.* **ROSE** *digs into her bag again.*)

ROSE. …need to write a note…

FRED CLOTALDO. Quickly.

(**ROSE** *produces a velvet case, from which she conspicuously and cautiously unsheathes an astonishingly ornate pen.*)

*(**FRED CLOTALDO** is instantly captivated.)*

FRED CLOTALDO. That implement...

ROSE. What about it?

FRED CLOTALDO. It's...very special...

*(**FRED** holds his hand out for the pen. Skeptically, **ROSE** hands it to him. He brandishes it with great flair.)*

ROSE. You hold it like you've held it before.

FRED CLOTALDO. Not possible.

ROSE. Why not?

FRED CLOTALDO. There's only one.

*(Beat. **ROSE** grows suspicious.)*

Sorry, where did you say you –

ROSE. A gift. From a woman. My mom.

*(Flabbergasted, **FRED CLOTALDO** turns to **ROSE**.)*

FRED CLOTALDO. Your mother.

ROSE. Yeah. It belonged to my deadbeat dickhead asshole deserting dad.

(They eye each other, examining one another's features, looking at one another's hands, posture, hairline, etc. They are both panicked at their findings.)

(Finally. The screech of the freight elevator. All look at it expectantly.)

(The door opens. It is empty. Inside, it glows, beckoning.)

SEGIS. Have a nice day.

(Lights out on the basement.)

*(**STELLA** and **ASTON** appear in different elevators [squares of light?]. They are both ascending to the 77th floor. They both wear good suits.)*

*(**ASTON** is texting on his phone. Projected [not spoken]:)*

"U R SOOO F-ING HOT
CAN'T STOP THINKING ABOUT U
THE SHEEN OF YOUR HAIR MOCKS THE
DAYLIGHT

YR GLIMRING EYES SHAME THE STARS
YR BREASTS ARE TWO RIPE...."

(He thinks a moment, contemplating the size of her chest.)

"...FIGS
WHICH MORTIFY ALL LESSER TREE FRUIT
I LONG TO STRIKE YR DEWEY SKIN..."

(He corrects the word "STRIKE" to "STROKE.")

"WHEN WILL U OPEN YR PETALS TO ME AGAIN?
HEART, ASTON"

*(He sends the message. **STELLA**'s phone beeps. She reads **ASTON**'s text, then thumb-types a reply. She is much more deft than he is.)*

"WHEN HELL FRZS OVR."

*(She sends the message. **ASTON**'s phone beeps. He reads, then replies.)*

"R U STILL ANGRY?"

(He sends. Beep. She reads and replies.)

"WHAT DO U THINK??"

(She sends. He replies.)

"HOW MNY TIMES DO I HAVE 2 APOLOGIZE?"
(It takes him a while to spell "apologize" correctly.)

(He sends. She replies.)

"ONCE WD BE FINE."

(She sends. He replies.)

"I'M SRRY."

(He sends. She replies.)

"NOT THRU YR PHONE, MYBE???"

(She sends. He replies.)

"U WON'T TALK 2 ME IN PRISON."

(He corrects "prison" to "person.")

(He sends. She replies.)

"NOT UNTIL U DELETE HER PIC."

(She sends. He looks sheepish. He waits a moment, then replies.)

"DONE."

(He sends. She replies.)

"BLLSHT."

(Both their elevator doors ding at the same time and open. They exit their respective spaces and see each other. They glare.)

STELLA. Coward.

ASTON. Cougar.

(In spite of themselves, they attack each other hungrily, groping and kissing and the like.)

(After a moment, they straighten themselves out.)

STELLA. Did you study the documents I gave you?

ASTON. Yes.

STELLA. Are you prepared for this / meeting, because if not

ASTON. Yes Stella, I am prepared for this meeting.

STELLA. Good. The usual. You shmooze I bruise.

*(**ASTON** smiles. They both move toward **BILL BASIL**'s office. **ASTON** knocks.)*

BILL BASIL. Come in.

(They enter.)

(The office is an enormous, gorgeous, sleekly designed space with enormous floor to ceiling windows and a tremendous view. The furniture is sexy and hyper-modern, but absurd and non-realistic.)

(One huge abstract painting hangs on the wall; it is of **BILL BASIL**, *but barely.)*

*(***BILL BASIL** *stands with his back to* **ASTON** *and* **STELLA**. *He wears an incredibly expensive, well-tailored suit.)*

(Various **ACCOUNTANTS** *also stand by, also wearing suits. They are busy and austere. They hold account- ing devices, and make constant calculations, conferring silently with one another.)*

*(***BILL BASIL** *does not turn around immediately.)*

ASTON. *(charming)* Good morning Bill how are you doing, is that a new shirt? Hey listen. Our stocks are still on the decline.

STELLA. We're thinking about dropping our Con-tel and Inter-core shares. Con-tel fell 5.3 percent last month. Inter-core fell 5 percent.

ASTON. No need to panic but it's getting a leeetle bit sticky / with the recent

STELLA. We have a net loss of a dollar thirty-one per share.

BILL BASIL. *(to accountants)* Kill them. Now.

(The **ACCOUNTANTS** *react to this, speaking quietly into their cellphones and text-messaging folks.)*

In their place?

ASTON. Well we have our eye on a bold little outfit called e-Village.

STELLA. It's hot.

ASTON. Scorching, really.

STELLA. But quiet.

ASTON. I got a tip from an old pal of mine from State U. Swell fella. Heck of a dancer. And boy can he barbecue –

STELLA. We need to act quickly.

*(***BILL BASIL** *picks up his phone.)*

BILL BASIL. Denise. Send Jerry Saks at e-Village a gift basket immediately. Sopressata, rosemary crackers, the works. And a note: " Let's talk. Bill Basil."

(He hands up.)

BILL BASIL. *(cont.)* Anything else?

STELLA. That's all for now, I believe…

ASTON. As always it's a total joy to see you. Oh, hey! Thanks so much for those bonuses. Completely unnecessary but so very much appreciated.

(A beat. **BILL BASIL** *turns and again faces the window.* **STELLA** *and* **ASTON** *look at each other quizzingly. They stand to leave.)*

(Finally, **BILL BASIL** *speaks.)*

BILL BASIL. Question:

What is the use of building an empire if there is no blood legacy to receive it?

(a beat)

ASTON. Um…

BILL BASIL. Sit down.

(They do. The **ACCOUNTANTS** *also sit, awkwardly and absurdly, as there are not enough chairs. They continue accounting.)*

Would either of you like a coffee? Tea? Seltzer with a squeeze of lime?

ASTON. Hey thanks, I'll have / a

STELLA. We're fine, thank you. What is this about?

BILL BASIL. My intentions.

STELLA. Regarding?

BILL BASIL. The future of this business.

STELLA. You're splitting the office into two heads. Aston as C.O.O and myself as C.E.O.

BILL BASIL. That *was* indeed the plan.

I understand you are both to be wed.

ASTON. Yes, we're looking at / places near

STELLA. *(coldly)* Plans are up in the air.

BILL BASIL. Then you well understand how intentions may be thwarted.

(**BILL BASIL** *snaps his fingers. The* **ACCOUNTANTS** *quickly hand him a folded newspaper clipping.* **BILL BASIL** *hands it to* **STELLA**, *and gestures for her to read it aloud.*)

STELLA. *(reading)* "Home and business collide, Sagitarius, as the Sun's transit of your chart's mid-heaven angle forces you to reflect upon a deep grievance you have with yourself. Planetary oppositions suggest that, if you value your professional reputation, you will give this some serious thought and then act. Lucky numbers 4, 7, 16, 25."

I don't understand.

(**BILL BASIL** *walks over to the painting of himself. He snaps his fingers again. With swiftness and efficiency, the* **ACCOUNTANTS** *exchange the painting for another abstract rendering: it is* **SEGIS**.)

(Then they return to their accounting.)

ASTON. Who is that?

BILL BASIL. My son.

(**ASTON** *and* **STELLA** *are shocked. A knock on the door.*)

Yes?

(**FRED CLOTALDO** *enters.*)

FRED CLOTALDO. Bill we've, oh, I didn't –

BILL BASIL. Come in, please.

FRED CLOTALDO. We have a situation….

BILL BASIL. One moment. The inevitable is upon us.

ASTON. When did you get a son?

BILL BASIL. Does the date October 19th, 1987 ring a bell?

ASTON. Wasn't that –

STELLA. Black Monday. The largest one day stock market crash in history. The Dow fell 23% in six hours, roughly $500 billion dollars. This company almost went under.

ASTON. You clawed your way back from oblivion. It was damn near miraculous.

(BILL BASIL gestures to **FRED CLOTALDO**. **FRED CLO-TALDO** *sighs heavily.)*

FRED CLOTALDO. At exactly 9:34am, Mr. Basil's wife went into labor. The market began its descent precisely one minute after. Mrs. Basil pushed for six hours. By the time the little boy emerged, the economy was a shambles. Tragically, Mrs. Basil did not survive the birth. Mr. Basil had not the tools to forgive the child for taking her from him. So he announced it had died as well. It had not.

ASTON. But…where…

FRED CLOTALDO. The child was placed into foster care until he was old enough to work. After that, we employed him in a position through which we could keep careful watch, though he would be rendered powerless.

ASTON. Not…

FRED CLOTALDO. Customer service.

STELLA. Oh Bill.

FRED CLOTALDO. This injustice has pressed most heavily on Mr. Basil's mind. Year after year, like a greedy sloth feeding on his guilt.

(BILL BASIL removes his nameplate "BILL BASIL, PRESIDENT," and ceremoniously replaces it with "SEGIS BASIL, PRESIDENT.")

BILL BASIL. One of the lone benefits of old age is the facility to acknowledge the untold pleasures of righting ones wrongs.

ASTON. But, sorry, if he has no experience, how can you expect / him to

BILL BASIL. Fred?

FRED CLOTALDO. The why's and wherefores are unimportant. You need only know that he must prove his competence. Please treat him with respect, and keep this confidential for now, for the sake of our investors. We don't need any unnecessary concern. If he is inept, he will be swiftly removed and you both will endure in his stead. Consider this a *trial* period.

STELLA. Bill…

BILL BASIL. I am placing   **FRED CLOTALDO.** He is placing
my –   his faith –

    *(***BILL BASIL** *glares at* **FRED CLOTALDO**, *who shuts up.)*

BILL BASIL. I am placing my faith in the heavens.

ASTON. Mr. Basil, with all due respect –

STELLA. This is suicide. Placing someone untrained, under-
qualified, completely un-vetted, at the head of a
multi-billion dollar…It's beyond reason. Especially with
the volatile business / climate

ASTON. Whoa whoa whoa. Let's not get ahead of ourselves
here. Let me pull some strings. I'll hook him up with
my buddies up north, get him into that accelerated
business / program over at

BILL BASIL. Thank you for your time. Leave now.

    (They do so, stunned. **FRED CLOTALDO** *remains.)*

Now. What is this "situation?"

FRED CLOTALDO. Security breach. Very minor. I'll tend to
it.

    *(***FRED CLOTALDO** *is about to exit.)*

BILL BASIL. Wait a moment.

    *(***BILL BASIL** *glares at the* **ACCOUNTANTS** *and clears his
throat.)*

ALL ACCOUNTANTS Oh.

    (The **ACCOUNTANTS** *exit.)*

BILL BASIL. Fred, I want you to plan my retirement party
in two weeks. On site. We shall make an official
announcement then regarding the new regime *(whom-
ever it shall be)*. In the meantime, I shall make myself
scarce.

FRED CLOTALDO. Very good.

    (a beat)

BILL BASIL. Fred?

FRED CLOTALDO. Yes Bill?

BILL BASIL. The tremors in my hand have gotten worse.

FRED CLOTALDO. What do you need me to do?

BILL BASIL. Nothing. I just wanted you to know.

FRED CLOTALDO. All right.

 (an awkward beat)

BILL BASIL. You may go now.

FRED CLOTALDO. Very well.

 *(**FRED CLOTALDO** exits.)*

 *(**BILL BASIL** is left alone in his office. He approaches the painting of his son.)*

BILL BASIL. Now perhaps you'll kindly extract yourself from my nightmares?

 *(Smoke fills the room. The **PAINTING OF SEGIS** comes alive. **SEGIS** is a punk rock star at a concert.)*

PAINTING OF SEGIS. Sucka
Who owns your kingdom now?
My name is Burden
Gonna ride you straight into the grave
How many ways can you be my slave

I am your liver spots
Your wiggling jowls
The steely stubble in your ears
The extra back flesh

I'm the tremors in your hands
I'm the pajamas you fold
I'm the inches you've shrunk
I'm the pillow in your coffin

Lay your head on me, daddy
Lay your head on me, sucka
Here is your thrown foal
He has stapled himself onto your soul
Yeah yeah yeah.

(**SEGIS** *enters the painting again. The smoke clears, lights back to normal.*)

(**BILL BASIL** *pours himself some tea. His hand is wracked with tremors.*)

(*Meanwhile, in the main office: another sleekly designed space, smaller, crowded, crammed with people, but still with excellent lighting and more modern yet absurd furnishings.*)

(*A bunch of extraordinarily hip and fantastically bored* **ASSOCIATES** *are "working" at their desks, which entails amusing themselves lethargically with paper-clip sculptures, phone cords-untanglings, white-board-drawing / erasings, and etc.*)

(**ROSE** *and* **CLAIRE** *sit in the reception area.*)

ROSE. It has to be some sort of labor violation…

CLAIRE. What?

ROSE. I mean the smell alone is a health hazard…

CLAIRE. Oh.

ROSE. But he COULD leave if he wanted to….

CLAIRE. The clinical term is "learnéd helplessness."

ROSE. There must be something we can do.

CLAIRE. Oh you mean from jail?

ROSE. They can't put us in jail, Claire.

CLAIRE. But they can keep a gross dirty madman in chains answering phones for twenty years. You know when I agreed to come I don't think I anticipated incarceration….

ROSE. "Agreed?" You BEGGED me to come.

CLAIRE. Well it sounded exciting! Infiltration of a massive corporation –

ROSE. SHHHHH!

CLAIRE. *(quietly)* Involving some mysterious package, the contents of which you won't tell me….

ROSE. Not "won't." Can't.

CLAIRE. You don't trust me –

ROSE. CREATE A DISTRACTION. *That* was your job. Not "annoy everyone."

CLAIRE. I'm not sure I fully comprehend the distinction.

ROSE. I need to think.

(They notice the **ASSOCIATES** *vlogging boredly.)*

CLAIRE. What's with all the little cameras?

ROSE. They're vlogging. Don't harass them.

*(***CLAIRE*** approaches the* **ASSOCIATES**.*)*

CLAIRE. *(proud, flirty)* We're going to the clink.

(The **ASSOCIATES** *do not cease vlogging.)*

The slammer.

(No response. **CLAIRE** *tries to get their attention.)*

The Big House. The Hoosegow. The jug. The brig. The can. The pen. The lockup. The pokey. The cooler. The haul. The probe. The gumrip. The kiosk. The birdhole. The mysterious T-zone. The cat-trap. The boogie base. The ho-square. The oiler. The valise. The Siberian holiday.

*(***FRED CLOTALDO*** enters.)*

FRED CLOTALDO. Change of plans. You're staying here.

CLAIRE. *(disappointed)* Oh.

ROSE. Why?

FRED CLOTALDO. You've been spared. In exchange for some temping.

*(***FRED CLOTALDO*** hands them some W4 forms.)*

W4 forms. Name address social etc.

(They fill them out, slightly confused, and return them.)

ROSE. And the man in the basement?

FRED CLOTALDO. He's gone.

ROSE. Escaped?

FRED CLOTALDO. Promoted. I'm sure you'll see him around.

(FRED CLOTALDO hands CLAIRE some sheets of paper.)

FRED CLOTALDO. *(cont.)* 600 copies. Stapled and collated. One in every box.

CLAIRE. *(happily)* But of course.

(CLAIRE disappears.)

FRED CLOTALDO. Does she follow you everywhere?

ROSE. She tries. She's very loyal.

(A beat. FRED CLOTALDO is eyeing ROSE intensely.)

ROSE. So. What should I do? Go fax some shit?

(A beat. FRED CLOTALDO still stares.)

That makes me uncomfortable.

FRED CLOTALDO. What. I'll stop.

ROSE. Good.

(A beat. He can't stop.)

You can't stop, can you.

FRED CLOTALDO. You look just like her.

ROSE. I look like myself.

(FRED CLOTALDO keeps staring. He tries not to but he can't.)

Okay, I don't know who you think you are, but you are wrong.

FRED CLOTALDO. Why are you here, then? For money? I have nothing. I live a modest / existence on my own

ROSE. I told you. I need to see him. Aston. I need to deliver the package myself. This…

(gesturing between them)

…this is just some unbelievably flukey cosmic uh, thing.

FRED CLOTALDO. You show up here with a vintage 1976 Oberon 1000 jewel-encrusted limited edition Flo-right with spring-ball tip and patented supple-grip casing, and expect me to believe it's a coincidence?

ROSE. I'm not acting.

FRED CLOTALDO. *Lying,* then. You're not a bike messenger.

ROSE. I am too!

FRED CLOTALDO. Where's your bike?

(**ROSE** *is busted.*)

I see you haven't inherited your mother's facility for guile....

ROSE. Which one is Aston's office?

FRED CLOTALDO. Mr. Martin is a high-level executive. He does not take meetings with just anyone.

ROSE. Dude! I gave you the pen!

FRED CLOTALDO. It was my pen!

ROSE. Prove it.

(**FRED** *points to a tiny place on he back of the pen.*)

FRED CLOTALDO. "F.C." FRED CLOTALDO.

(small beat)

I *made* it.

ROSE. You "made" it? Like, forged it?

FRED CLOTALDO. I was an engineering student at M.I.T... in training for the Special Weapons division of the CIA. Office supplies.

ROSE. So it's a weapon?

FRED CLOTALDO. It's many things.

ROSE. That's kind of awesome. Why the heck aren't you over there building killer post-its or whatever?

FRED CLOTALDO. None of your business. Now excuse me, I have work to do. And so do you.

(He hands her a paper. She reads it.)

Your temporary assignment is to help Ms. Strong. She just fired ANOTHER assistant...

ROSE. *(sickened)* Strong. *Stella* Strong?

FRED CLOTALDO. You know her?

ROSE. No.

FRED CLOTALDO. Good. Find a suit for the love of God.

(He exits.)

(We watch as the **ASSOCIATES** *vlog at their desks)*

(NOTE: These are completely disaffected youths. Even when their language is seemingly invested, their tone and their bodies all convey a studied disinterest and lethargy. All engagement should be dripping with sarcasm and irony. AIR QUOTES.)

ASSOCIATE ONE. Yo yo, it's J-dawg in the hizzy, welcome to my vlog yo…

(He sings a popular hiphop song, replacing the lyrics with various iterations of "my job sucks" or "I hate my job.")

ASSOCIATE TWO. I just watched all of Gossip Girl online. Then I made this necklace out of thumb tacks, sweater lint and an ink pad. I feel like I'm just like, waiting to be fired. WORK FAIL.

ASSOCIATE THREE. So, like, I know a lot of you guys out there are going through stuff like pay cuts and hour reductions and layoffs and whatevs. But like, here, we just hired *two* new people! AND some dude from the basement is getting a promotion. We're performing terribly and Basil's a fossil, so WTF? Any thoughts? Hit up my comments yo.

ASSOCIATE FOUR. *(the himbo-geek)* So, I haven't had bacon in a good like, three to four years? And I went down to the cafeteria for lunch? And I got like, a steak wrapped in bacon? It tasted like turd. But I liked it.

(Lights out. The basement. Darkness.)

*(***SEGIS** *stares at nothing for a bit.)*

SEGIS. Rigorous facilitators march through celebrated corridors.

(He stares at nothing for a bit.)

Calamitous fallacies may arouse base cravings in the ignorant fanatic.

(He stares at nothing for a bit.)

SEGIS. *(cont.)* My voice talking to no one.

Here's the sound of language.

Here's the sound of my own lips throwing futile spirals at the wall.

(From the chute falls a handful of loose cooked macaroni and some lettuce leaves.)

(He shoves the macaroni into his mouth, gagging a little.)

Cold.

(He shoves the lettuce into his mouth, gagging a little.)

Warm.

(Then, an apple falls. He takes a huge bite.)

Weird.

(Almost immediately, he grows woozy. The air fills with a low ringing.)

Whoa. Headrush...too much talking...

(A sonorous blow shakes the earth. The lights flicker with it, and the machines move closer to **SEGIS**.*)*

(He nearly loses his balance.)

Razorblading my eyes...my throat squeezing...

(Another sonorous blow, louder. The lights flicker, the machines move closer to **SEGIS**. *He nearly falls again. He grabs the apple.)*

Fermented, maybe? My tongue is bulky...

*(***SEGIS***'s hands are forks.)*

Forks...

(A final sonorous blow, enormous and vibrant. The lights flicker, the machines are upon **SEGIS**. *He drops the apple and falls, passing out.)*

(After a long moment...shriek of gears, etc. The freight elevator door opens. **BILL BASIL** *and* **FRED CLOTALDO** *emerge with two* **SECURITY GUARDS**. *One of them checks* **SEGIS**'s *pulse.)*

BILL BASIL. Good lord…dreadful…who approved these conditions?

FRED CLOTALDO. You did, Bill.

BILL BASIL. Ah.

(**BILL BASIL** *examines his son.*)

He appears deceased.

FRED CLOTALDO. It's just the drugs.

BILL BASIL. *(moved)* I've never been this close to him.

(beat)

In review: when he awakens, you shall tell him his life down here is defunct, and his true station is President.

FRED CLOTALDO. Yes.

BILL BASIL. And if he fails, you shall send him back down here and tell him his time above was all a dream.

FRED CLOTALDO. If that is your wish.

BILL BASIL. I want this to work, Fred.

FRED CLOTALDO. It will.

BILL BASIL. He's got the blood of a leader coursing through his veins…

FRED CLOTALDO. He's a good kid.

(A beat. No one moves.)

Shall we?

BILL BASIL. I'm going to linger a bit. If you don't mind.

FRED CLOTALDO. Very good.

(The **SECURITY GUARDS** *drag* **SEGIS** *into the freight elevator and disappear with* **FRED CLOTALDO**.*)*

*(***BILL BASIL** *lingers behind. He walks around, examining things. He touches an old machine and a layer of grime comes off on his finger. He frowns in distaste.)*

(He kicks at the rusted chain.)

(He tastes a little macaroni, then spits it out.)

(Finally, he sees the press clippings hanging on the wall, along with his photos.)

(He examines them. He's in awe. He singles out one clipping.)

BILL BASIL. "Bill Basil keeps his management on a tight leash…" Huh.

(He singles out another.)

"Basil's employees are like drones in his massive anthill – efficient, unsparing, and utterly dedicated." Well I must concur…

(He singles out another.)

"Basil handles his behemoth of a company like a multi-headed hydra; when he lops off one unprofitable asset, two lucrative ones sprout up in its place."

(He looks at others, reading them to himself. Incredulous.)

Are these *all* about me?

Could he have known??…No. But…perhaps, embedded in his bone marrow…we are one blood, after all… he is a Basil.

(He examines the items on SEGIS's desk: a notepad; a highlighter; a newspaper; the phone.)

(BILL BASIL notes the phone receiver is a lighter color where SEGIS had been gripping it for years.)

(The phone rings. BILL BASIL jumps.)

(It rings again. BILL BASIL freezes.)

(It rings again. BILL BASIL answers.)

CustomerservicehowmanyIhelpyou?

(Lights down.)

Interlude

(A stylized montage of workers doing office things, set to music. Perhaps we see the passed-out **SEGIS** *being shaved and prepared.)*

*(Lights up on **BILL BASIL**'s office. **SEGIS** is slumped at Bill's desk with his head on the desk and his hand wrapped around a coffee mug. He is shaven, hair clean and short and slicked back, and he wears an expensive suit.)*

*(**FRED CLOTALDO** stands over him)*

FRED CLOTALDO. ...any minute now...

*(**FRED CLOTALDO** touches the office supplies on **SEGIS**'s desk, absently, admiringly, starting with the stapler.)*

Stylex Pro 6000 punch-quick platinum with speed release. Beauty.

(He touches a lamp.)

Velva-glow Lumina series with advanced dimming, everlong halo-bulb, and European wattage regulator.

(He lifts a pencil and smells it. He gasps and remembers something.)

*(He reaches into his pocket and removes the pen **ROSE** gave him. He examines it.)*

Mint condition!

(a beat)

I have a daughter.

*(He regards **SEGIS**.)*

Lose a child, gain a child....

*(to **SEGIS**)*

Well, you got what you dreamed, I suppose. Power, fortune...a real father.

He was a visionary, you know. He had this native dominance, this...air of inevitability.

Haven't seen him that way in years.

Maybe this is exactly what the company needs. A jolt of energy. Something to yank us up from the muck of this putrid economy.

(CLAIRE knocks and enters.)

CLAIRE. *(brightly)* Hello, boss! I've separated all the third quarter spreadsheets into weekly folders and I set up a system of color-coding based on the day, for example Mondays are blue, get it, blue Mondays, Tuesdays are tangerine because of the alliteration, Wednesdays are lavender because I was born on a Wednesday and lavender is my favorite color, Thursdays are green because of Mean Green Thursday, which I made up, and Fridays are yellow because they are scared of the weekend.

Also, I re-bradded all of the invoice packets from the last four years because apparently SOMEONE had used the wrong size brads and all the pages were loose, see now they don't flap around!

(She demonstrates.)

What's wrong with that person?

FRED CLOTALDO. Too much sake. Have you seen your friend?

CLAIRE. Yes! They made her dress like a dork. She's working for that really pretty lady with the heels and the hair and the frown, like the perpetual frown…

FRED CLOTALDO. What name is she going by?

CLAIRE. Her real name. Rose.

FRED CLOTALDO. Rose. What is she like?

CLAIRE. What do you mean?

FRED CLOTALDO. Just. In general.

CLAIRE. Um. Loud? Twitchy? Fast eater? I don't know her that well. She moved in a few months ago. Found my roommate listing on Craigslist. Oh, she told me to tell you she's still waiting for that big meeting with Mr. Martin.

FRED CLOTALDO. Perhaps you can keep that last bit of information to yourself.

CLAIRE. Is that part of my job? To keep confidences?

FRED CLOTALDO. Yes.

CLAIRE. Then consider it done! La la la la. Okay I need to go systematize the envelopes in the supply closet... WHAT A MESS....

(She exits happily, slamming the door.)

(He tries out the name.)

FRED CLOTALDO. Rose.

(He shakes his head.)

Horrible name.

(SEGIS pops awake.)

SEGIS. Son of a whore!

FRED CLOTALDO. Good afternoon, Mr. Basil.

(SEGIS focuses his eyes. He turns and sees the huge windows with the amazing view. He clutches the desk and screams as though he is falling to his death.)

SEGIS. AHHHHHHGGGGKKKKAHHHHH!!

FRED CLOTALDO. They're just windows! See? Glass...

(FRED CLOTALDO taps the glass with his knuckles.)

SEGIS. WHAT AM I LOOKING AT?

FRED CLOTALDO. It's the outside. It's sky, it's buildings. We're 77 stories up.

SEGIS. WE'RE WHAT???!!!

FRED CLOTALDO. I'm afraid you fell asleep at your desk, Mr. Basil. You must have been having a nightmare.

(SEGIS frantically feels for his beard.)

SEGIS. Where is the rest of my face? What the hell's in my hand?

FRED CLOTALDO. Coffee. Probably cold by now. Let me take that from you.

(FRED CLOTALDO carefully removes the coffee mug from SEGIS's hand.)

(SEGIS finally notices his clothing.)

SEGIS. How did this get on me? When was I naked?

FRED CLOTALDO. I understand this must be completely disorienting, Mr. Basil...

SEGIS. Why do you keep calling me that? Give me some flipping answers, please.

FRED CLOTALDO. Calm down. You...this is awkward. Um, so your father read this horoscope...

SEGIS. I don't have a father.

FRED CLOTALDO. Yes you do. It's Bill Basil.

SEGIS. *(scoffing)* The President. Right.

FRED CLOTALDO. Former President. I'm sure he will do a MUCH better job explaining everything, but all you need to know is that he's handing the company down to you as his next of kin. Now, I'll be serving as your advisor until / you get on your feet

SEGIS. Whoa whoa whoa. Say that again.

FRED CLOTALDO. I'll be your advisor –

SEGIS. The other part.

FRED CLOTALDO. He's handing the company to you.

SEGIS. The company. To me.

FRED CLOTALDO. Yes.

SEGIS. You're serious.

FRED CLOTALDO. As death.

SEGIS. Why.

FRED CLOTALDO. It's your birthright. You're his son.

SEGIS. Who was I before?

FRED CLOTALDO. His employee.

SEGIS. Who's in customer service?

FRED CLOTALDO. We have a posting on Craigslist.

SEGIS. And whose office is this?

FRED CLOTALDO. Formerly, Mr. Basil's. Currently, yours.

SEGIS. Prove it.

(**FRED CLOTALDO** *gestures to the name plate on the desk.*)

SEGIS. *(cont.)* This is my name. These are my letters. "President." My name and the word "President."

FRED CLOTALDO. I'll be right back. Make yourself comfortable.

*(**FRED CLOTALDO** disappears.)*

*(**SEGIS** takes a moment to register everything.)*

SEGIS. My last name is Basil.

*(**SEGIS** laughs hysterically.)*

My father is one of the most successful, most feared men in the entire corporate sphere.

Myfatherisbillbasil myfatherisbillbasil myfatherisbillbasil myfatherisbillbasil myfatherisbillbasil myfatherisbillbasil.

My father is Bill Basil, and this is his office.

(He looks around…)

(Everything in the room becomes more vibrant somehow…alive…the sky is a brighter, more psychedelic shade of blue…the furniture is breathing somehow…)

(incredulous) This is MY office.

Mine.

(He looks at the desk.)

My pencils. My lamp. My phone.

(He picks up the phone receiver, uncertainly. He presses a button, Someone on the other end answers.)

Oh, hello. HowcanIhelp –

*(**SEGIS** halts himself, clears his throat, and puts on his best Presidential voice, still a bit unsure of himself.)*

This is Segis Basil. President. I would like, um…. a gigantic platter of the most sumptuous foodstuffs known to mankind. Now.

(He hangs up the phone. A knock on the door.)

*(**SEGIS** reaches for the door as though his foot is chained to the desk, not realizing he is free.)*

(A gigantic platter of the most sumptuous foodstuffs known to mankind lays at the doorstep. The food is colorful and weird, barely recognizable.)

(SEGIS slides the food into the room, slams the door, and hungrily dives into the platter on the floor, smearing food all over his face and hands.)

(He speaks with his mouth full.)

SEGIS. *(cont.)* Mmmmm.....

My food!

My floor!

My company!

Why did he give this to me?

(He eats more, and contemplates.)

He's been waiting.

Testing me.

The phones

The darkness

The buzzing

The stench

The isolation

The macaroni

Any man who can endure the basement

has the strength to run a corporation.

(He glances down at his foot. It is chain-free. He wiggles it.)

No chain.

(He then climbs the furniture in ecstasy.)

Ha ha! What else can I do?

(He sees the electronic stapler on the desk. It glows, it pulses.)

(SEGIS grabs a few sheets of paper and slides them into the stapler.)

(The stapler lights up as it staples the pages.)

SEGIS. *(cont.)* Ah!

They staple themselves!

(SEGIS begins stapling many things, wildly.)

The power to make pages staple themselves!
Is this what it means to be a ruler???!!

(He staples the curtains. He staples the painting. He staples stuff to the walls. He staples stuff to the furniture. He staples madly, recklessly.)

HA HA HA!!

Will I split the walls with my power?

SPLIIIIT!

(The wall splits. A lit mirrored bar is revealed, filled with colored liquor bottles, crystal glasses, bowls of lemons and limes, shakers, an ice bowl with tongs, other bar implements, little bottles of tonic and coke, tea bags, a small fridge, etc.)

THANK YOU, DAD!

(A knock on the door. SEGIS grabs the stapler and slides it into the front of his pants.)

Enter!

(FRED CLOTALDO enters with the ACCOUNTANTS.)

FRED CLOTALDO. Ah, I see you've found the bar. Mr. Basil, these are your accountants.

(The ACCOUNTANTS begin calculating and buzzing about. SEGIS is confused a moment…then he realizes.)

SEGIS. Ohhhh…. The ants on my anthill!

(The ACCOUNTANTS become ants.)

FRED CLOTALDO. Ladies and gentlemen, this is Segis Basil, the new president of BASIL ENTERPRISES. We'll be introducing him more formally at / Bill Basil's retirement party

SEGIS. *(to FRED)* You're fired.

FRED CLOTALDO. Mr. Basil, you need me.

SEGIS. You're the shitheel who kept me chained to the desk for most of my life!

(Realization.)

And LIED to me about not having a father!

FRED CLOTALDO. It wasn't my choice. I was under strict / orders to

SEGIS. Get him out of here.

FRED CLOTALDO. Be careful, young man...this might all be a dream....

SEGIS. But it's MY dream. And you're fired from it. GET OUT OF MY FACE!

*(**FRED CLOTALDO** exits.)*

*(**SEGIS** jumps up on his chair and spins wildly around.)*

What is the first thing I will do as President?

I'll whip my employees into shape!

*(A whip falls from above. **SEGIS** grabs it and brandishes it.)*

ACCOUNT-ANTS! Give a report.

*(The **ACCOUNT-ANTS** scramble to give their report.)*

ACCOUNT-ANTS. *(in unison)* For the current fiscal year, um, we report a net income of \$2.31 billion on \$25.33 billion in revenue, down from a net income of \$3.43 billion on revenue of \$28.65 billion last year –

*(**SEGIS** whips the **ACCOUNT-ANTS**. They scurry around, climbing on the walls and each other, like ants.)*

SEGIS. What else?

ACCOUNT-ANTS. *(in unison)* Um, the, the key decline driver in the quarter was our initial acquisition of N-com dot com, which should see an operating income jump of 85% to \$155 million in the coming year –

SEGIS. SELL IT!

ACCOUNT-ANTS. *(in unison)* Oh. That would not be wise –

SEGIS. This company is a multi-headed hydra! Lop off one unprofitable asset and two lucrative ones will sprout up in its place!

ACCOUNT-ANTS. *(in unison)* But, well, N-com is profitable –

SEGIS. ENOUGH!

(**SEGIS** *whips the* **ACCOUNT-ANTS**. *They scurry around even more frantically, shouting into their cellphones.*)

ACCOUNT-ANTS. Sell! Sell! Sell!

(They continue.)

(**CLAIRE** *enters.*)

CLAIRE. Are you the new boss?

SEGIS. *(roaring)* Who are you?

CLAIRE. The temp.

SEGIS. POUR ME A SELTZER!

(He whips at her.)

CLAIRE. *(pouring)* Yikes! Okay!

(He knocks the seltzer out of her hand.)

SEGIS. POUR ME ANOTHER SELTZER!

CLAIRE. All righty!

(**CLAIRE** *continues to pour seltzers and place them around the room for the duration of the scene.*)

SEGIS. ACCOUNT-ANTS! Next order of business…bulldozing the competition. Send six hundred bulldozers over to the competition and MOW IT DOWN.

(*He whips the* **ACCOUNT-ANTS**. *They scurry and climb about, yelling into their cell-phones.*)

ACCOUNT-ANTS. Mow! Mow! Mow!

(**ASTON** *knocks and enters. He carries a bunch of papers.*)

ASTON. Whoa. Um Hello Mr. Basil. Allow me to be the first in management to welcome you to your new position –

SEGIS. LEASH!

(A leash flies in. **SEGIS** *hurls the collar at* **ASTON**.*)*

*(***ASTON** *fastens the collar onto his own neck.)*

ASTON. Thank you. My name is Aston Martin. I've been with the company for six years. I was personally responsible for 30 percent of last year's income ratio. Ooh, snug. I think you'll find me a sound advisor, a compelling spokesperson, and a pretty congenial AGGK!

*(***SEGIS** *tugs violently on* **ASTON**'s *leash.)*

ASTON. What the heck!

SEGIS. I keep my management on a tight leash...

ASTON. I believe that's just a metaph – AGGK!

*(***SEGIS** *yanks again.)*

Sorry. At any rate, I'll be needing approval for these budgets –

*(***SEGIS** *grabs the stack of papers and a rubber stamp.)*

*(***SEGIS** *reads each page carefully, and then stamps it and tosses it into the air.)*

SEGIS. Hmmmm. NO!
Ahhhhmmm. YES!
NO!
YES!
No, no no no no. Absolutely not. Forget it. Never. NERVER.

(The **ACCOUNT-ANTS** *scramble to collect the papers.)*

ASTON. I'm not sure / this will be

*(***SEGIS** *points to various* **ACCOUNT-ANTS**, *snapping his whip.)*

SEGIS. You! Climb that wall! Draw that curtain! Sharpen that pencil! Lick that wound! Burn that book! Eat that dust! Pluck that eyebrow! Sew that seed! File that nail! Spread that rumor! Disconnect that number! Roll that stone! Wag that dog! Shoot that shit! Skin that cat! Hang that ten! Spin that wheel! Make that grade!

Sound that fury! Jump that jack! Cook that goose!
Chop that liver! Rain on that parade! Throw oil on
that fire! Shake that money maker!

*(The ACCOUNT-ANTS madly set about doing all this.
All is frenzy.)*

*(One of the ACCOUNT-ANTS tries to shake another
ACCOUNT-ANT's money maker as SEGIS watches.)*

*(Suddenly, an earsplitting alarm sounds. A huge elec-
tric sign reading "SEXUAL HARRASSMENT" begins
to blink.)*

*(The SEXUAL HARRASSMENT GUARDS storm in and
whisk the ACCOUNT-ANT away.)*

*(CLAIRE hands SEGIS a seltzer. He knocks it out of her
hand.)*

CLAIRE. Oh okay.

(STELLA enters. She is instantly horrified.)

STELLA. Mr. Bas – good lord.

*(SEGIS is alarmed by her beauty. He moves toward her,
dragging ASTON behind him.)*

ASTON. Mr. Basil, this is Stella Strong, the – AGGK!

STELLA. Why is my fiancée on a leash?

ASTON. It's okay Stella, I got this one –

SEGIS. WHO THE HELL ARE YOU?

STELLA. The woman who will save this company from ruin.
Am I to understand that you've just sold N-com dot
com, our most profitable asset?

SEGIS. NONE OF YOUR FREAKING BUSINESS!

*(The lights suddenly go out. The room is running on
an eerie reserve power source, which gives everything a
spooky blue glow.)*

SEGIS. What happened?

STELLA. The primary shareholder of N-com is the power
company, Mr. Basil. We lose them, we lose our lights.

(**SEGIS** *ponders this a moment. He yanks on* **ASTON**'s *leash.*)

ASTON. AGGK!

SEGIS. Go fix that.

ASTON. Certainly.

(**ASTON** *bounds out the door.*)

(*A beep.* **STELLA** *glances down at her cellphone.*)

STELLA. And now I see you have wrecking crews assembled in six financial districts around the globe. Without permits. The lawsuits alone will bankrupt us. Now if you don't mind, I'm going to issue a stop work order on ALL of them.

(*She types into her phone.*)

SEGIS. You are beautiful.

(**STELLA** *sighs deeply, still typing.*)

STELLA. Four years at Harvard and three at Wharton and I STILL have not found a way to respond to that kind of remark without emasculating my superiors so I'll just say this, and feel free to receive it with whatever degree of irony you feel comfortable: "Thank You For The Compliment."

SEGIS. (*suddenly desperate*) I feel like something inside me is dying when I look at you.

(*He moves closer to her, hungrily. She holds her own, not moving.*)

STELLA. (*suddenly fierce*) I'm on to you, Bucko. You're as transparent as a sheet of air. The old man lets off a whiff of dementia and you smell that shit from seventy stories down, come skulking up here and start scrapping the joint so you can cash out and buy a resort island in Micronesia. Well don't you think for one hot second / I'm going to let you

SEGIS. (*suddenly desperate*) Your words aren't little wips… they're heavy crashing things…I love you. I love you.

STELLA. What…

SEGIS. Jerk me into your undertow. Suck the air from me. Fill my mouth with your salt. I am feebled.

STELLA. *(in his thrall)* Uh…

(The room becomes an ocean.)

(ALL THE SELTZERS IN THE ROOM glow blue, and begin to fizz loudly, volcanically.)

STELLA. What's happening?

Am I doing that?

SEGIS. We both are.

STELLA. My gosh…

You see me.

SEGIS. I do.

STELLA. *(suddenly vulnerable)* You see the me I am

Not the me I need to be

SEGIS. I do

*(**SEGIS** lunges at her, ravenously. **STELLA**, aroused and confused, backs away. She staggers out the door, slamming it in his face.)*

(The seltzers stop fizzing.)

(a beat)

*(**SEGIS** vaults into a rage. He hurls everything off his desk. Then he notices the **ACCOUNT-ANTS**, who are timidly watching him.)*

SEGIS. YOU'RE FIRED!

ACCOUNT-ANTS. *(in unison)* What did we do?

SEGIS. GET OUT GET OUT GET OUT!!

*(He whips them frantically. The **ACCOUNT-ANTS** scramble out, climbing all over each other, etc.)*

CLAIRE. Thank goodness. They were skeeving me out –

SEGIS. MORE SELTZER!!

*(**CLAIRE**'s bottle is empty.)*

CLAIRE. Back in a jiffy.

(She slips out.)

(SEGIS is out of his mind frustrated.)

SEGIS. Why did she run from me? I kept my manager on a tight leash, I whipped my employees into shape, I bull-dozed the competition...I'M DOING EVERYTHING RIGHT!

(All the appliances in the room glow menacingly, the sky changes color outside, and the room darkens. Perhaps foreboding music plays.)

(SEGIS is frightened. The fax machine beeps. A fax comes in.)

(SEGIS slowly moves to the machine. He retrieves the fax. He reads.)

"To Segis Basil.

From Bill Basil.

Subject: You."

(A jolt of excitement passing through SEGIS.)

Dad...

(The fax machine beeps again, still menacingly. A second page comes in. SEGIS reads.)

"Son: I had hoped your noble blood would trump your unfortunate upbringing. I can't tell you what a disappointment this has been."

(to the air.)

I'm sorry, Dad...I'm not sure where I screwed up...

(reading)

"You were handed a multi-billion dollar enterprise overnight, one for which you did not lift a digit. It could disappear just as quickly. Neither of us wants that."

(to the air)

I know...I can do better...just tell me how....

(reading)

SEGIS. *(cont.)* "In review: Consider this a warning. Do not abuse the extraordinary privilege you've been given."

(to the air)

But how do I not do that?

(silence)

I don't know what I'm doing!

(silence)

Hello?

(Silence. SEGIS works himself up again.)

Why did you bring me up here? Whose dream is this?

(The fax machine beeps again. A third page comes in. SEGIS reads.)

"The dream is your own. Do with it what you will. End transmission."

(to the air)

WHAT THE HELL DOES THAT MEAN? DAD!!!!

(Nothing.)

(Suddenly, SEGIS grips his heart.)

Ow! What the. OWW!

(Huge pain. He writhes from it. This is Big Deal Pain, a pain he's never felt before. He is doubled over. He moans.)

(ROSE knocks and enters. She is wearing a corporate casual ensemble, vastly different from her scrubby messenger outfit.)

ROSE. Mr. President Sir, I wondered if I could trouble you – are you okay?

SEGIS. LEAVE ME ALONE!!!

(ROSE squints at SEGIS.)

ROSE. Holy moley. It's YOU.

SEGIS. Go away.

ROSE. I mean they said you got a promotion, but President –

SEGIS. ARE YOU DEAF?

(recognizing her) The bike messenger. In a suit.

ROSE. It's not mine. Listen, Head Honcho and all that, I need you to get me a meeting with Aston Martin. The future of this company depends on it.

SEGIS. I don't give a shit about the company. I want that woman back.

ROSE. Then why did they put you in charge?

SEGIS. I have no idea. I want that woman back…

ROSE. Whose idea was it to promote you?

SEGIS. My father's.

ROSE. Who's your father?

SEGIS. My father is B-b-bill Basil.

ROSE. Shut up!

SEGIS. He's a visionary. Single-handedly saved this company when the market was shredding itself. He's a great man.

ROSE. Right. Taught you how to ride a bike too, huh.

*(**SEGIS** grabs his heart again. More pain.)*

SEGIS. No…

ROSE. Sang you songs to help you sleep. Carried you on his shoulders. Saved your report cards. Took you camping. Cooked you scrambled eggs.

*(**SEGIS** is writhing.)*

What is up with you?

SEGIS. My heart…

ROSE. Should I call someone?

SEGIS. I WANT THAT WOMAN! GET ME THAT WOMAN!

ROSE. WHAT WOMAN??

SEGIS. THE ONE WITH ALL THE WORDS!

ROSE. I can't help you, man….

SEGIS. Please…

*(He grabs **ROSE** desperately, imploring.)*

(The earsplitting alarm sounds from earlier. The "SEXUAL HARRASSMENT" sign begins to blink.)

ROSE. What the heck??

*(**FRED CLOTALDO** enters with several guards. They tear **SEGIS** off of **ROSE**.)*

FRED CLOTALDO. Are you all right?

ROSE. I'm fine, geez...

*(**FRED CLOTALDO** whips out a syringe and injects something into **SEGIS**'s behind. **SEGIS** falls.)*

ROSE. What was that? What did you do?

FRED CLOTALDO. He's dangerous, it was necessary.

ROSE. He's completely harmless!

FRED CLOTALDO. You call attempted rape harmless? You're welcome, by the way.

*(They drag **SEGIS** out the door.)*

ROSE. Rape? That was a hug!

FRED CLOTALDO. Unsolicited physical contact is a strict no-no. The policy was designed for your protection.

ROSE. Oh BS. You're sweeping your trash under the rug.

FRED CLOTALDO. Be that as it may.

ROSE. Mom was totally right about you.

FRED CLOTALDO. What the hell does that mean?

ROSE. Nothing.

FRED CLOTALDO. You know I've had just about enough of your attitude.

ROSE. Isn't that cute, how you think I give a crap.

FRED CLOTALDO. Maybe you should.

ROSE. And maybe YOU should have stuck around to raise me.

FRED CLOTALDO. I was forcibly deposed!

ROSE. Not according to her.

FRED CLOTALDO. No surprise there.

(Lights come on.)

FRED CLOTALDO. *(cont.)* Great, lights. You know how I found out she was pregnant? I dug through the trash in the bathroom and found the test.

ROSE. You didn't want a kid!

FRED CLOTALDO. You're right. Not with her. But after I found that test, I dropped out of M.I.T. and got a job. THIS job. Came home one day and found all the locks had been changed. And here I still am.

ROSE. She said you left us.

FRED CLOTALDO. Of course she did. Her pride was like a Chinese dragon. Vibrant, ornate, and hideously writhing. Could never admit she was wrong.

ROSE. Whatever. She's dead now.

FRED CLOTALDO. What? When?

ROSE. Last month. Cancer.

FRED CLOTALDO. Oh no. I'm so sorry.

ROSE. Actually she's totally alive. She asked me to tell you that if we ever met up.

FRED CLOTALDO. Oh.

ROSE. She lives in a retirement community in the pine barrens. She has a boyfriend. A lawyer. They go to Montenegro every winter.

FRED CLOTALDO. Ah.

ROSE. No really, she's dead.

(a beat)

To you, I mean.

FRED CLOTALDO. Go burrow in a snowbank and freeze to death.

ROSE. DON'T TELL ME WHAT TO DO!

*(**ROSE** storms into the closet, thinking it's an exit.)*

FRED CLOTALDO. That's a closet!!

*(**FRED CLOTALDO** is about to exit but runs into **CLAIRE** carrying a case of seltzers.)*

CLAIRE. Oh hello. The new boss just got dragged away. He asked for seltzer earlier. I got a whole case. Heavy!

FRED CLOTALDO. Put it over there.

CLAIRE. Yes sir! You know I have to say I am remarkably good at my job. I excel at following commands to the letter AND I have stupendous organization skills. PLUS I am not above menial tasks and I sure do enjoy the feeling of accomplishment one gets / when one

FRED CLOTALDO. Excuse me.

CLAIRE. But of course.

(**FRED** *is about to exit.*)

Um boss?

FRED CLOTALDO. Yes?

CLAIRE. Is the new boss going to the clink?

FRED CLOTALDO. Not if we don't press charges...

CLAIRE. "Press charges?"

FRED CLOTALDO. We can't sustain any bad publicity.

CLAIRE. "Bad publicity"?

FRED CLOTALDO. Just keep it quiet. Goodbye.

(**FRED** *exits, finally.*)

CLAIRE. Electrifying!!!

(**ROSE** *emerges from the closet.*)

ROSE. Claire!

(**CLAIRE** *jumps, startled.*)

CLAIRE. Ah!

ROSE. What are you doing??

CLAIRE. Temping! What are YOU doing?

ROSE. Infiltrating!

CLAIRE. From a closet?

ROSE. I thought it was an exit. It's like a whole apartment in there. It's got rooms, a kitchen...Why are you fetching seltzer?

CLAIRE. It's my job.

ROSE. Your "job" is to help me.

CLAIRE. But I like temping.

ROSE. You *like* being a corporate flunkie?

CLAIRE. I'm keeping confidences. I'm organizing things. I feel important.

ROSE. Claire! They are evil! They will KILL YOUR SOUL!

CLAIRE. *(pointed)* At least they confide in me. If one is loyal to a someone, it's only fair to expect something in return. Now I don't mean to be rude, but I have a TON of things to do. Bye!

(CLAIRE exits.)

ROSE. Shoot shoot shoot! I need to think…

(ROSE disappears back into the closet.)

(longish beat)

(STELLA enters curiously. She surveys the wreckage…the mauled food, the seltzers, the papers everywhere, etc.)

(Then touches some objects with reverence and confused longing.)

(She picks up a seltzer. She closes her eyes. She tries to make the seltzer fizz and glow blue. It does not. She tries again, not sure what she's doing.)

(ASTON enters, rubbing his sore neck. STELLA quickly drinks the seltzer.)

ASTON. OUTRAGEOUS. The hell was the old man thinking? I mean he wouldn't spoon-feed his life's work into the mouth of a lunatic unless he stood to gain from it…Well I suppose family run businesses DO average about 6 percent more profit and 10 percent more value than regular ones…maybe he was trying to give the quarter a little boost.

(He massages STELLA's shoulders.)

Ah well. Thank god that little horror show is over. What now, darling? Should we call a press conference announcing the new regime?

(**STELLA** *says nothing. She is not even listening.*)

ASTON. *(cont.)* You're uncharacteristically mute.

STELLA. Sorry, what?

ASTON. Um, so we're about to be handed a multi-billion dollar corporation on the verge of collapse? Wanna tune in for a bit?

STELLA. *(flustered)* Sorry. I'm just a little. That was very upsetting. The way he made people jump...

ASTON. It was completely demoralizing.

STELLA. That too....

(**ASTON** *watches her carefully. Realizes.*)

ASTON. Oh my god. You have a crush.

STELLA. What? Don't be moronic. I was just taken aback by his...whatever. Raw passion.

ASTON. Are you serious?

STELLA. It was powerful! And undeniable. Don't dismiss it, Aston. He could be an asset to us, at some point...

ASTON. He's an ANIMAL.

STELLA. But that kind of um. *Initiative,* it doesn't grow on trees. With my coaching, who knows? I did wonders for you.

ASTON. Uh, don't compare me to a village troll. I got here by hard work and personal magnetism.

STELLA. Oh get real. Without me in a room you fall apart like a pair of synthetic running shorts.

ASTON. And what happens when *I'm* not in the room?

(small beat)

STELLA. *(reluctant concession)* Nothing. Because I have no talent for obsequiousness.

ASTON. Precisely. Now enough of this, darling. Why not let's grab lunch, have a glass of wine, figure out the next few days...

STELLA. Could I see your phone please?

ASTON. Why?

STELLA. I just want to check something.

ASTON. Stella. I deleted it. I told you. Now get your coat.

> (**ASTON** *picks a seltzer off the floor. He drinks it.*)
>
> (**STELLA** *holds out her hand for the phone.*)
>
> (**ASTON** *ignores it and picks up another seltzer.*)
>
> Gosh, I'm so thirsty. Why am I so thirsty?

STELLA. Aston. The phone.

ASTON. My word should be sufficient.

STELLA. It should, shouldn't it.

ASTON. I don't have it on me.

> (*She continues to hold out her hand. He continues to ignore it and drink the seltzers.*)

ASTON. Why do you insist on giving one photo such import? The way I see it, each photo is a rung on a ladder that leads directly to you, my darling.

STELLA. I'm quite familiar with the serviceable truths you manufacture to keep yourself deluded, Aston, but why not spare *me* that embarrassment?

> (**ASTON** *storms toward the door.*)

Where are you going?

ASTON. To get my phone, Stella. Do I have permission?

> (*He exits.*)
>
> (**ROSE** *enters from the closet, embarrassed.* **STELLA** *shouts, surprised.*)

ROSE. Sorry...I thought it was an exit. Have you been in there? It's like an apartment!! It's got rooms, / a kitchen

STELLA. Rose. I need you to do something.

ROSE. Okay.

STELLA. Something potentially outside the range of your assistant duties.

ROSE. Okay...

STELLA. Mr. Martin – my fiancé – has a photograph of a woman on his phone. I need you to delete it.

ROSE. Um. I'm / not sure

STELLA. It's for the good of the business. Aston and I will soon be heading this company. If the phone were misplaced or lost, and someone were to discover that photo…Well we certainly don't need a scandal before we've even begun.

ROSE. Of course.

STELLA. It shouldn't be too difficult. Mr. Martin's powers of perception are often eclipsed by his vigilant narcissism…which of course makes him stunning in the sack. The needy ones always are…

ROSE. Um…

STELLA. *(vaguely disgusted with herself)* We've probably covered every square inch of this place naked… He's a pleaser, you know. And he loooooves to be dominated.

ROSE. Um, great! Okay, so. The photo?

STELLA. Right.

ROSE. Right. What does it look like?

STELLA. No idea. My last assistant caught him fawning over it and saw fit to enlighten me, catty thing. Just look for some tarty bimbo, I'm sure you won't be far off.

He'll be back any moment. I'll return shortly.

(STELLA is about to leave. She pauses at the door.)

I understand the younger Mr. Basil made advances towards you.

ROSE. Um…

STELLA. How was that?

ROSE. …I don't know.

STELLA. Hm.

(STELLA exits thoughtfully.)

(ROSE sits in a chair and panics. She grabs her package.)

ROSE. No no no! How can I look at him with her name in my eyes? "Every square inch??" Oh god. Could things POSSIBLY be any worse?

Rose. Lock it up. Stuff it in the trunk and slam the lid. He's a blowtorch but you're a steel beam. Take that heat.

I can't.

You CAN. Take it and turn it back on him. That's what you're here for, right?

Yes. Okay. Melt the man. Press down on him like a grilled sandwich. MAKE IT HAPPEN, ROSE...

(ROSE's knees are shaking. She loses her will.)

OH GOD!!...And this PLACE!!

(She considers the package in her hands.)

Rose. Remember what you have in your hands. A red-hot four-alarm scandal. You hold all the cards. YOU have the power.

Yes. Yes.

(ASTON enters, holding his phone.)

ASTON. I feel like a nine-year-old...

(He immediately recognizes ROSE. He reacts as though all the little scaffoldings inside him just collapsed. The air is completely charged between them.)

You.

ROSE. Yeah. So?

ASTON. What are you doing here?

ROSE. Temping. I'm Stella's assistant.

ASTON. WHAT? Since when?

ROSE. About 9am.

ASTON. Baloney. You're not qualified. You despise the corporate sector with every fiber of your being.

ROSE. Just trying to make a buck, like everyone else.

(He eyes her.)

Don't give me that look...

ASTON. Rose…

ROSE. And don't say my name like you know how to fold it. You lost your right to that tone years ago.

ASTON. Months.

ROSE. Who's counting?

ASTON. Seven.

ROSE. We make choices and we live with them. And yours seem to have paid off. How much did that haircut set you back?

ASTON. It's part of the job.

ROSE. And the wife? I'll bet she cost / an arm

ASTON. We're not married yet.

ROSE. Is *she* part of the job too?

ASTON. I don't want to talk about Stella.

ROSE. You know they're calling you both the "merger of the decade…"

ASTON. It's just publicity.

ROSE. Of course. Preserve your image at all costs. You haven't changed. But why would you? It's your nature. Spraying yourself with German colognes, inviting yourself into the foyers of chirpy widows to quote "sell them hairbrushes"…three months later you've got a new scooter….

ASTON. I was fifteen!

ROSE. Same shtick, different price tag. Oh, nice name by the way. Aston. I like that it has the word *ass* in it.

(He smiles, big and genuine.)

ASTON. God, I missed you.

(She's disarmed. He touches her.)

ROSE. Don't do that.

ASTON. Okay…

(He doesn't stop. She is in a trance.)

ROSE. This isn't you, Reggie…

ASTON. Don't call me that. Of course it's me. The *new* me.

ROSE. You're not a shark...you're some other harmless charismatic animal.

ASTON. ...A gecko.

ROSE. Sure.

ASTON. What about you? Who are you pretending to be? You put on pink lipstick...you wore terrible shoes...

ROSE. They're not mine...

ASTON. You could have just called to say you're sorry...

ROSE. I wanted to see you. Wait. What? Why would *I* be apologizing to *you?*

ASTON. For throwing me out.

ROSE. You were CHEATING.

ASTON. I was NOT cheating. I slept with Stella AFTER you kicked me out.

ROSE. She was sending you steamy emails! You REPLIED! You said STEAMY things!

ASTON. She was my boss! I was trying not to jeopardize my work relationship!

ROSE. So telling her to stop would have been out of the question...

ASTON. Yes! At the time, yes! Things were very delicate....

ROSE. And now you're cheating on her too. Isn't that adorable.

ASTON. What are you talking about?

ROSE. The chick on your phone. The one driving your betrothed batty.

(small beat)

ASTON. How do you know about that?

ROSE. Betrothed wants ME to get rid of the photo.

ASTON. Ha. That's funny.

Be my guest.

(ASTON hands ROSE his phone.)

ROSE. Wow, okay. Where is she?

ASTON. Hit Menu, then Extras, then scroll down to the second page.

(**ROSE**'s *hand won't stop shaking. Frustrated, she attempts to steady it with her other hand while she types.*)

ROSE. (*as she's hitting buttons and scrolling*) Hey here's a thought...if you're gonna take a lover, you might wanna be a LEEEETLE more discreet about...

(*She finds the photo. She gasps a little.*)

Huh.

When, when did you take this?

ASTON. The weekend we got trashed in Vegas.

ROSE. Where are my pants?

ASTON. You gave them to Elvis.

ROSE. I don't remember that.

ASTON. I don't remember much either. Except how crazy I was about you.... You had that short pixie haircut...

ROSE. I hate that haircut.

ASTON. I love that picture.

ROSE. Why are you keeping it?

ASTON. Why do you think?

(*Magic fingers again.* **ROSE** *submits.*)

ROSE. (*small voice*) Tell her? When she comes back?

ASTON. Tell her what?

ROSE. You want a demotion? You're breaking off the engagement? You have a real name?

ASTON. I can't do that.

ROSE. You can. Just open your mouth / and say the words

ASTON. It's too late. Things are in motion.

ROSE. Then stop them...

ASTON. Basil's handing the company over to us.

(*Small beat.* **ROSE** *breaks away.*)

ROSE. Congratulations.

(**ROSE** *begins to tap buttons on* **ASTON**'s *phone.*)

ASTON. What are you doing?

ROSE. Where the heck is delete?

ASTON. Give it to me!

(They struggle for the phone. Naturally, STELLA enters at the most compromising moment.)

STELLA. Is this a bad time?

ROSE. Um, actually, no. He has something to tell you.

STELLA. Oh?

(Small beat. ROSE looks to ASTON to make a decision. He turns to STELLA.)

ASTON. Your assistant here, um, what was your name again?

ROSE. R-rose.

ASTON. Rose, yes. She is, she has a...

*(**ASTON** looks to **ROSE**. He gives her a pleading face. She recovers.)*

ROSE. Oh. Um. God how embarrassing. Mr. Martin – that's MY phone. We have the same phone. I'm such a dope. I grabbed at your phone accidentally, then realized it was the wrong one. But THAT one is mine.

ASTON. So where's MY phone?

ROSE. I don't know.

ASTON. Then how do you know THIS one isn't mine?

ROSE. Because that's me. In the photo. See?

*(**ROSE** grabs the phone and shows **STELLA**.)*

An old boyfriend took it...

STELLA. You had man-hair. Very flattering.

ROSE. Thanks. Sorry I couldn't take care of that other business...

STELLA. No worries.

*(**STELLA** approaches **ASTON** and begins to stroke him like a pet. This is clearly an act of aggression against **ROSE**. **ASTON** takes it like a reptile.)*

*(**ROSE**, in agony, turns to leave.)*

STELLA. Wait a moment...

> (**ROSE** *stops. And waits.*)
>
> (**STELLA** *continues stroking.*)
>
> (*after a moment:*)

You may go on lunch now.

ROSE. Great.

STELLA. Oh by the way. That suit is appalling. And that lipstick looks like it's made of sugar. Bill Basil's retirement party is in two weeks...Could you try to make yourself look a little less...cheap?

> (*small beat*)

ROSE. Will do.

> (**ROSE** *scurries off.*)
>
> (*A beat.* **ASTON** *and* **STELLA** *glare at each other.*)

ASTON. You didn't have to do that to her.

STELLA. I am so tired of propping you up. And I am so tired of being the shrew. And, I live with the daily knowledge that no matter how much more competent, experienced, and intelligent I am than you, we are in the exact same position on the food chain here. So you can either hold my hand all the way to the bank, or you can wallow here in your own shit with your boxers at your ankles. But hear this: I WILL NOT let you destroy this for me.

> (*She exits.*)

ASTON. STELLA!!

> (*He follows her. Lights down.*)

End of Act One

ACT TWO

(PROJECTED: The associates' vlogs. More supreme ennui.)

ASSOCIATE ONE. Holla. Some trippy shit up in this hizzy, mofos. What the whats all I gots to say. Peace.

ASSOCIATE TWO. ...he was SOOOO rad! He tore it up! That NEVER happens. People here are robots. This guy was like. The opposite of robots.

ASSOCIATE THREE. ...and HALF the accounting staff was laid off. Who's next? What happened to Wild Basement Dude? Thoughts? Hit up my comments.

ASSOCIATE FOUR. So I like, hacked into the financial data? And like, management got these HUGE bonuses? But we're getting a wage freeze? And I'm like, WOW. That blows. 'Cause now I gotta get RAGEFUL.

*(Lights up on the basement. **BILL BASIL** is still answering phones. He looks miserable.)*

BILL BASIL. I'msosorrytohearyou'vebeenhavingtroubles....

(Squawking is heard through the phone line.)

I'm not sure what I can do for you at this time....

(Squawking through the phone line.)

There is no manager. You're speaking with the President.

(More squawking through the phone line.)

Well perhaps you should seek therapy for that.

(More squawking through the phone line.)

Hold on a moment. I have another call.

*(**BILL BASIL** carefully hangs up the phone. It rings immediately.)*

CustomerservicehowmayIhelpyou.

(beat)

BILL BASIL. *(cont.)* Fred, thank goodness.

(beat)

Oh dear.

(beat)

Well I suppose that's that. Bring him back down.

(BILL BASIL *hangs up. He places his head in his hands miserably.)*

What have I done?

(A PHOTO OF BILL BASIL *begins to speak.)*

PHOTO OF BILL BASIL. You can answer that one for your-self…

BILL BASIL. *(lashing out)* He crushed my happiness in one tiny bloody fist. Who gave him that power?

PHOTO OF BILL BASIL. He was innocent.

BILL BASIL. Nonetheless, I rectified the situation. He failed.

PHOTO OF BILL BASIL. How did you expect him to succeed?

BILL BASIL. By his wits. Same as I.

PHOTO OF BILL BASIL. You had training. You had exposure. You climbed up through the ranks.

BILL BASIL. I came from squalor. Same as he.

(The **PHOTO OF BILL BASIL** *laughs.)*

PHOTO OF BILL BASIL. You've lost it, Bill…You're a wash-out…a lame duck…

(BILL BASIL *grabs the photo and tears it up.)*

BILL BASIL. And you, my good fellow, are dust.

(ANOTHER PHOTO OF BILL BASIL *laughs.)*

ANOTHER PHOTO OF BILL BASIL. You couldn't pull the com-pany out of despair. You're not the man you were…

(BILL BASIL *tears that photo to bits as well.* **ANOTHER PHOTO OF BILL BASIL** *speaks.)*

Your empire is withering Bill…and so are you…

(Laughter echoes around him. **BILL BASIL** *begins to tear apart all the photos and articles of him, in a frenzy. Like an animal.)*

(The laughter dies. **BILL BASIL** *catches his breath. His hand shakes. He stops it.)*

(The phone rings. **BILL BASIL** *unplugs the cord from the wall.)*

(The freight elevator begins to whir. Quickly, **BILL BASIL** *grabs for some materials to disguise himself. He looks absurd and hilarious. He hides.)*

*(***FRED CLOTALDO, CLAIRE** *and the* **GUARDS** *arrive in the elevator. The* **GUARDS** *carefully place* **SEGIS** *back in his seat.)*

FRED CLOTALDO. Be gentle…watch his feet…the chain please…

*(***FRED CLOTALDO** *notices* **BILL BASIL.***)*

FRED CLOTALDO. Bill, what…?

BILL BASIL. I wanted to see him awaken.

FRED CLOTALDO. Why?

BILL BASIL. I don't know.

FRED CLOTALDO. …the outfit…?

BILL BASIL. I'm incognito…

FRED CLOTALDO. Perhaps you should stand in the shadows. For your own safety.

BILL BASIL. Of course.

*(***BILL BASIL** *hides in the shadows.* **SEGIS** *stirs.)*

SEGIS. *(mumbling)* …you're all fired…

BILL BASIL. What did he say?

FRED CLOTALDO. Just mumbling…

SEGIS. …father…why have you forsaken me….

FRED CLOTALDO. He said –

BILL BASIL. I heard that one…

CLAIRE. So when do we tell him? That he lost everything.

FRED CLOTALDO. We don't.

CLAIRE. But he'll certainly remember…

FRED CLOTALDO. We say it was a dream.

CLAIRE. Why?

FRED CLOTALDO. Because that's what Mr. Basil Senior wants.

CLAIRE. I don't get it.

FRED CLOTALDO. All you need to know is, nothing ever happened.

CLAIRE. Okay.

FRED CLOTALDO. And he is NOT, I repeat, NOT your boss.

CLAIRE. Right. *You* are.

FRED CLOTALDO. Correct.

CLAIRE. So what should I be doing?

FRED CLOTALDO. Why not push that fax machine around the room.

CLAIRE. Okay! Watch me go…la la-la…

(**CLAIRE** *begins pushing the ancient fax machine around and around the room.*)

(**SEGIS** *suddenly pops awake, as before.*)

SEGIS. Take a memo!

(*He takes a moment to survey his surroundings. Checks the phone in his hand. Etc.*)

My head…how did I get back down here?

FRED CLOTALDO. Good afternoon…

SEGIS. Where are my Account-ants?

FRED CLOTALDO. What are you talking about?

SEGIS. Where's my suit? Where are my seltzers? Why aren't you fired?

CLAIRE. Loony-bird…

SEGIS. Why is this chain around my ankle again? Goddamn it, I'm the President of BASIL ENTERPRISES. and I want some answers!

(**CLAIRE** *and* **FRED CLOTALDO** *laugh gaily.*)

FRED CLOTALDO. Perhaps you DREAMED you were the president.

SEGIS. No, everything changed...my father is Bill Basil. He gave me the company.

FRED CLOTALDO. Why would he do that?

SEGIS. I don't know.

FRED CLOTALDO. I assure you, you've been fast asleep since lunch. Perhaps you were ill...you were very restless...

SEGIS. He sent me a fax.

CLAIRE. Oh weird. Me too.

(CLAIRE and FRED CLOTALDO laugh gaily once again.)

FRED CLOTALDO. I know this is a huge disappointment for you...

SEGIS. But...the wall split...And a woman.... she turned the room into an ocean...

CLAIRE. How does someone turn a ROOM into an ocean?

(She winks knowingly and extravagantly at FRED CLOTALDO.)

FRED CLOTALDO. The *fevered* mind is a lively architect...

(FRED CLOTALDO hands SEGIS some aspirin and water.)

Here. This will bring your temperature down.

SEGIS. ...but she was real...and my father....

(SEGIS grabs at his heart.)

OW! See? That's ACTUAL pain.

FRED CLOTALDO. Of course it is. Drink up...

SEGIS. If it was a dream then what happened to my hair?

FRED CLOTALDO. Lice.

SEGIS. Oh. I *was* kind of itchy...

(SEGIS looks around and notices his articles are in shreds.)

Did I do that?

FRED CLOTALDO. Who else?

(**SEGIS** *is totally miffed.*)

I have a meeting.

SEGIS. But the hurting...

FRED CLOTALDO. The pain you feel in dreams is never lost, even when waking.

(*A beat. Pointed.*)

Neither is the pain you inflict. Remember that. Good-bye, son.

SEGIS. I'm not your son.

FRED CLOTALDO. (*exploding*) Fine, yes, I know, all right?

(**FRED CLOTALDO** *plugs* **SEGIS**'s *phone back into the wall.*)

(*The* **GUARDS, BILL BASIL,** *and* **FRED CLOTALDO** *enter the freight elevator and are about to depart when* **SEGIS** *catches sight of* **BILL BASIL.** *Their eyes meet.*)

SEGIS. Do I know you?

BILL BASIL. No.

(*The freight elevator doors close.*)

(**CLAIRE** *continues to push the fax machine around.*)

SEGIS. What does that even mean, to dream?

(*to* **CLAIRE.**)

Are you dreaming you're pushing an ancient fax machine around a room? Or am I dreaming you're pushing an ancient fax machine around a room? Or am I dreaming that you're dreaming you're pushing an ancient fax machine around a room?

CLAIRE. No idea. Would a "thank you, Claire" have been so difficult? Or how 'bout a "good job, Claire!" Noooooo...it's "push that around, Claire." "Clean up that mess, Claire." "Lie to people, Claire." Doesn't loyalty mean anything to anyone?

SEGIS. And what is this pain? Is it dream-pain? If so, why does it feel so real?

CLAIRE. I'm versatile. I'm committed. Everything runs more smoothly with me around. So how is it that I'm invisible?

SEGIS. What about the fireflies in my eyes, the acid in my veins? What about the joy of bending others to my will? That feels real too...

CLAIRE. Maybe if I'm invisible enough, people will start to notice what a good job I'm doing.

SEGIS. I felt alive. For the first time in my life. How do I get it back? Should I try dreaming again?

CLAIRE. Sure.

(**SEGIS** *puts his head down on the desk. He tries to dream. He groans.*)

SEGIS. Not working.

(**SEGIS** *jumps up and tries a different position. Doesn't work.*)

Not working.

(**SEGIS** *puts one hand on the phone and one hand on his stapler, trying to get back to the dream.*)

(*He tries. Fails.*)

(*He tries. Fails.*)

(*He tries. Fails.*)

CLAIRE. Former Boss could you not slam the phone several times now?

(**SEGIS**, *unaware, grabs the phone and is about to slam it onto the desk. He stops.*)

SEGIS. (*genuinely bewildered*) How did you know I was going to do that?

CLAIRE. (*matter of fact*) Pattern recognition.

(**CLAIRE** *encourages* **SEGIS** *to try sleeping again. She sings him a little lullaby. It works.*)

Interlude

(Once again, a stylized montage of workers doing office things, set to music. However, what was once an efficient machine is now breaking down. The office has become a bed of unrest.)

(Projected: "TWO WEEKS LATER...")

*(Lights up on **BILL BASIL**'s office. A white line splits the room, the floor, the desk, and the windows in half. On one half of the desk is a nameplate that reads "STELLA STRONG, C.E.O." On the other half is a nameplate that reads "ASTON MARTIN, C.O.O.")*

*(The room is in complete shambles. A rectangular patch darkens the wall where the painting of **SEGIS** used to hang.)*

*(**ASTON** is alone and miserable. He addresses the lamp as if it were **ROSE**. He is formal and charming.)*

ASTON. Hello! Haven't seen you around the office lately... Well, you look great. That's a fantastic outfit ...

I'm fantastic, thanks for asking. No, the rumors are completely false. Stella and I are getting along maddeningly well. Wedding plans are at full throttle.

(He falters. Beat. Gear change.)

Why didn't you throw me under the bus with Stella? Where have you been for two weeks? Why can't I get you out of my flippin' head? Where is my phone?

(A beat. Quiet, genuine.)

I'm sorry. I'm sorry. I'm sorry. I'm sorry.
I love you.

*(**STELLA** enters. The two glare at one another and sit in their respective chairs.)*

*(After some quiet fuming, **ASTON** picks up the phone.)*

Hello Vincent, it's Aston Martin over at BASIL ENTER-PRISES? Yes, how are you, great. Listen, I wanted to know about those shares for Dink Inc., have they gone down at all? ...mm-hm...mm-hm...okay, lets buy thirty thousand. Fantastic. Talk to you soon.

*(He hangs up. **STELLA** picks up her phone and dials.)*

STELLA. Hi Vinny, it's Stella. Hold off on Dink Inc. for now. Because I said so. Fine.

(She hangs up.)

*(***ASTON*** *fumes some more. A beat.* ***STELLA*** *picks up the phone.)*

Denise, can you get me a box of blue Sharpies? I would really love if you could – Oh just do it. Now.

(She hangs up. ***ASTON*** *picks up his phone.)*

ASTON. *(smile in his voice)* Denise, hi sweetheart. Yeah, hold off on the Sharpies? Oh, you are a complete doll! Give Artie and the twins big hugs for me…M'kay…m'buh-bye.

*(***ASTON*** *grins.* ***STELLA*** *fumes.)*

*(***FRED*** *enters. Sounds of revolt and unrest outside.)*

ASSOCIATE ONE. *(offstage)* What up with the bonuses, yo?

ASSOCIATE TWO. *(offstage)* Are our jobs in danger?

ASSOCIATE THREE. *(offstage)* Where's the dude from the basement?

ASSOCIATE FOUR. *(offstage)* The cafeteria steak tastes like booty!

FRED CLOTALDO. *(out the door, the party line)* We're in a recession! Cutbacks are in everyone's interest! Thank you for your patience!

(He shuts the door.)

(calmly) So sorry to bother you both…just thought I'd give you a heads up that your employees out there are a tad um. Vexed. Apparently they've been letting word slip to that effect. Someone from Forbes called yesterday looking for an official statement on the quote-unquote "charade."

ASTON. Listen Fred, we appreciate your visit but we were just about to get ready for Bill Basil's retirement party.

STELLA. *(to* **FRED***)* You may explain to Mr. Martin that he is not to speak for me regarding my afternoon plans or anything else.

ASTON. You may tell Ms. Strong that it is commonly known her attendance is required at the function and therefore I made an informed assumption.

STELLA. Tell Mr. Martin one cannot make informed assumptions. To "assume" means to conjecture without proof.

ASTON. You can thank Ms. Strong for the linguistics lesson.

STELLA. You can tell Mr. Martin I'll do so as long as he's an imbecile.

ASTON. You can tell Ms. Strong to go eat a crap sandwich.

STELLA. Fred, I'm off to get my gown from storage. Please text me if anything comes up.

ASTON. Fred, I'm off to get my suit from the cleaners. Please text ME if anything comes up.

(They exit. More sounds of unrest outside.)

(Door closes. **FRED CLOTALDO** *lets out a huge breath. He locks the door. Then he knocks on the closet door.* **BILL BASIL** *emerges, wearing pajamas.)*

FRED CLOTALDO. You catch all that?

BILL BASIL. I've caught everything that has transpired in this room for the past two weeks. Every. Last. Thing.

FRED CLOTALDO. Well. We have a problem. We have several, actually. I'm sure you've heard our stocks have plummeted...

*(***BILL BASIL***'s hand begins to tremor violently. He tries to ignore it and stares out the window.)*

(a beat)

BILL BASIL. Before this building was a building it was a graveyard. Did you know that?

FRED CLOTALDO. No.

BILL BASIL. The headstones were removed and it was sold to a real-estate company in the 20's for an exorbitant amount. They had no idea what they had bought. When they broke ground and unearthed the bones, they were already steeped in debt and had to make a quick decision; should we exhume the bodies and track down the families, or should we lay down the foundation and pave over them? I don't need to tell you which they chose.

I've built my home on a pile of corpses, Fred. I remember thinking at the time it was an apt metaphor for the kind of career I wanted.

(A beat. Tremors.)

I've made a terrible mistake. I could have faced my disease like a man. Held my position until my own body tore it from me. Instead I was weak.

FRED CLOTALDO. You couldn't have predicted this. Aston and Stella were more than qualified...

(The tremors start again. **BILL BASIL** *tries to stop them.)*

Damn it! The ignominy. I can't let it end like this.

FRED CLOTALDO. Nothing has been done that can't be undone.

BILL BASIL. And who is left to do the undoing? No one.

FRED CLOTALDO. That's not true.

(a beat)

BILL BASIL. What are you suggesting?

FRED CLOTALDO. Prove yourself courageous in the face of devastation. Go out fighting.

BILL BASIL. You don't mean reclaim the company...

FRED CLOTALDO. That is precisely what I mean. Just for a moment. As a gesture of primacy. After all you've put into this ship, you damn well better be at the helm when it sinks.

BILL BASIL. Look at me, Fred. I can't hold a cup of goddamn coffee!

FRED CLOTALDO. Then I'll hold it for you.

BILL BASIL. I pride myself in being the kind of man who can recognize when his girders have rusted...

(**FRED CLOTALDO** *approaches* **BILL BASIL.**)

FRED CLOTALDO. Twenty-two years we've known each other. Each year another grey hair on my head. Look.

(*He points to a grey hair.*)

The Rauchbaum incident.

(*He points to another.*)

The Leeds and Miller bloodbath of '86.

(*He points to several others.*)

Christmas '98, in and out of court with Hastings...our seven-month dispute with the state....

(*He points to a few more.*)

Black Monday...when you handed that baby boy to me and told me it hurt too much to look at him, and I promised you I'd watch over him, give him language. Did I not?

BILL BASIL. You did.

FRED CLOTALDO. And look.

(**FRED CLOTALDO** *gestures to a few more non-grey hairs.*)

Here, here, here, here... About forty hairs that haven't gone.

These are for the Great Plummet of '09.

You can do this, Bill. My scalp is your witness.

(*A long beat. They share a moment.*)

BILL BASIL. Goddamn it Fred. We shall add my bones to the pile, then. Where is my vintage charcoal pin-striped Armani?

(**FRED** *smiles.*)

FRED CLOTALDO. In the vault.

BILL BASIL. Get it for me.

FRED CLOTALDO. Right away.

> (**FRED CLOTALDO** *is about to exit, as* **BILL BASIL** *surveys the wreckage.* **FRED CLOTALDO** *turns back.*)

I've, I've recently found out I have a daughter. Foulmouthed, bad-tempered...but there's something to her, like a... I don't know.

BILL BASIL. And how does this affect me?

FRED CLOTALDO. *(taken aback)* It doesn't.

BILL BASIL. You may go.

> *(small beat)*

> (**FRED CLOTALDO** *exits.* **BILL BASIL** *takes* **ASTON** *and* **STELLA**'s *nameplates and throws them in the trash. He removes his nameplate from his pajama pocket and places it squarely on the desk.*)

> *(He takes a deep breath and smiles.)*

Big Bill is back.

> *(In the basement.* **CLAIRE** *is still pushing the fax machine around.* **SEGIS** *is in a daze, still with one hand on the phone and one hand on his stapler, still trying to get back to the dream. He begins to nod off.)*

> *(**CLAIRE** is frazzled and hysterically exhausted.)*

CLAIRE. ...my legs are like a jar of preserves without the jar...no one told me how many times around I'm supposed to go...I'm not complaining! I'm not complaining! But like, when is lunch? I don't need much. Baloney sandwich cream soda paper napkin bag of chips...little patch of sunlight...maybe a tiny fountain nearby...okay, forget the fountain, I'll just sit by the faucet in the ladies room...

> *(The freight elevator squeals. The door opens. Out skulk the hip and bored* **ASSOCIATES**. *They are SOO over it. Every word out of their mouths is dripping with ironic sarcasm. Air quotes abound.)*

(They look around the room. The smell hits them.)

ASSOCIATES FOUR & THREE. WHOA!

ASSOCIATE TWO. STANK-CENTRAL!

ASSOCIATE ONE. Yo, hammer, what up.

CLAIRE. What the cow are you doing here? Have you come for me?

ASSOCIATE ONE. Where's da badass at?

CLAIRE. What?

ASSOCIATE TWO. Like, the progeny, um

CLAIRE. Who?

ASSOCIATE ONE. Progizzle, my nizzle.

CLAIRE. Oh, I'm sorry, I don't speak Hipster.

ASSOCIATE THREE. Bill Basil's son?

CLAIRE. Oh yes, I know where he is. What do you need him for?

ASSOCIATE TWO. Motivation.

ASSOCIATE FOUR. We're like, recruiting him?

ASSOCIATE THREE. We wanna oust Strong and Martin.

CLAIRE. Oh. Well I'm sorry but I am not permitted to divulge his whereabouts.

ASSOCIATE THREE. Aren't you the temp?

CLAIRE. I was, yes….

ASSOCIATE FOUR. They like, demoted you?

CLAIRE. This isn't a demotion! This is a very important job!

(noticing **SEGIS***)*

ASSOCIATE TWO. Look…

(The **ASSOCIATES** *approach* **SEGIS**, *who is still asleep. They watch him, fascinated.)*

CLAIRE. Hello, excuse me…

ASSOCIATE ONE. He so chillaxed.

CLAIRE. *(grabbing a pad and pen)* Could I please have your names and your departments?

ASSOCIATE TWO. He looks like a wizard.

ASSOCIATE THREE. Wonder what he's dreaming…

(Suddenly, the basement disappears, along with the others. **SEGIS** *and* **BILL BASIL** *are alone, wearing smoking jackets and puffing on pipes. They are seated in leather arm chairs and are reading two copies of* The Financial Times.*)*

(after a moment)

BILL BASIL. Did you read about Micron Media?

SEGIS. Chapter seven. A shame.

BILL BASIL. Couldn't survive the choppy waters. Unlike you.

SEGIS. Indeed.

(They puff and turn the page.)

Kendall Waters from Em-phase called. Wants to have dinner next Thursday.

BILL BASIL. I just read about them…lost their biggest shareholder…

SEGIS. Cut their holdings by half.

BILL BASIL. Did you drop the guillotine? Send over some biscotti with a note, "Piss off"?

SEGIS. No. I called him. Asked if he wouldn't mind meeting.

*(***BILL BASIL*** *is surprised.)*

BILL BASIL. That's not the way I would have handled it.

SEGIS. Things are different now, pops.

(a beat)

BILL BASIL. I'm proud of you, son.

SEGIS. Good.

(They puff and read.)

(Suddenly, the chairs and pipes and jackets and newspapers disappear, and we are back in the basement.)

(The **ASSOCIATES** *are still staring.)*

ASSOCIATE ONE. Ring ring.

*(***SEGIS*** *awakens with a start and answers the stapler.)*

SEGIS. CustomerservicehowmayIhelpyou.

ASSOCIATE FOUR. Are you like Bill Basil's sprog?

SEGIS. His what?

CLAIRE. Oh dear…

> (**CLAIRE** *slips off into the freight elevator and shuts the door.*)

ASSOCIATE THREE. His golden larva. Hump dumpling. Brattislavia. Ugray-atray.

SEGIS. One sec…

> (*Whips out a thick book called* ABRIDGED GUIDE TO MODERN HIPSTER. *Leafs through it furiously.*)
>
> (*leafing, mumbling*) …Ugray-atray… Ah! "Offspring." "Am I Bill Basil's offspring." Once…in a dream…

ASSOCIATE TWO. Are you an evil genie?

SEGIS. (*flipping through book*) Eeeeviiiilllll…. geeeenieeeee….

ASSOCIATE TWO. We heard you like, shut down the power grid in the entire city with like, your mind.

SEGIS. Oh. No. Sorry. I'm just the customer service guy.

ASSOCIATE FOUR. Um like Basil disappeared? And like the new management? Is like out of control?

ASSOCIATE THREE. We need a regime change.

ASSOCIATE ONE. SAVE US, MOFO!! WE GOT NO MARKETABLE SKILLZ!

SEGIS. I can't help you. Go find Bill Basil. He's the visionary.

ASSOCIATE ONE. Basil? He's a pathetic douche!

> (**SEGIS** *roars and grabs something officey and threatens* **ASSOCIATE ONE** *with it. Then he threatens the other* **ASSOCIATES**.)

SEGIS. How dare you. That man is a god. Do you know how many people out there would KILL to be employed by him? Just to be in the same BUILDING as him is a privilege. You don't know how lucky you are.

ASSOCIATE ONE. Wow. You got mad respect for your pops. That's deep.

SEGIS. I told you. I'm not his son. I only dreamed I was.

(The ASSOCIATES look at each other knowingly.)

(A Forbes magazine falls from the sky and lands at their feet. ASSOCIATE ONE hands it to SEGIS.)

(On the cover is an austere photo of BILL BASIL with the headline "THE SECRET BLOOD LEGACY.")

"Blood legacy…" What is this?

(The ASSOCIATES read from the magazine.)

ASSOCIATE THREE. "According to an unnamed source at BASIL ENTERPRISES, the troubled Basil has an unknown son whom he has"

ASSOCIATE TWO. "kept hidden for over twenty years, secretly working up plans to hand over the"

ASSOCIATE FOUR. "company to him at a propitious moment."

ASSOCIATE ONE. That's you, dawg.

(He reads.)

SEGIS. Holy smokes…It *wasn't* a dream…I'm totally Bill Basil's son! HA!! MyfatherisBillBasil Myfatheris – Wait a second. How did I get back down here?

ASSOCIATE THREE. Um, he fully betrayed you, homes.

ASSOCIATE TWO. Sold you out like a teen pop star.

ASSOCIATE FOUR. There are rumors? That he like, set you up?

SEGIS. He wouldn't do that to me. I'm his flesh and blood. There's definitely an explanation. Like. He. Misplaced paperwork, or. Even heroes make mistakes. Fred taught me that.

Oh dang! I totally fired him. I'll fix that. Once I'm President Part Deux.

(The machines glow and buzz.)

THE ASSOCIATES. DUDE!

SEGIS. I will right all wrongs.

(*The machines glow brighter and buzz louder.*)

THE ASSOCIATES. DUUUUDE!

SEGIS. I will make my father proud. I WILL TAKE BACK THIS COMPANY.

(*The whole room glows and buzzes.*)

(*Something bubbles up inside* **SEGIS** *body. He feels it.*)

Whooo, HA!!! DON'T WAKE ME UP!! I FEEL ALIVE AGAIN!

What now?

ASSOCIATE ONE. Weapons

ASSOCIATE TWO. Vehicles

ASSOCIATE THREE. Media

ASSOCIATE FOUR. Uniforms

SEGIS. NOTHING!

I have a feral mind, and I'm not afraid to use it.

We will dream of what we need when we need it!

LET THE SUBVERSION COMMENCE!

(*The* **ASSOCIATES** *cheer boredly as* **SEGIS** *roars like an animal and maybe throws some shit or breaks something. They all storm over to the freight elevator.*)

(**SEGIS** *pushes the elevator button. They wait. And wait.*)

(**SEGIS** *pushes the button again. They wait. And wait.*)

Who exactly are we deposing?

ASSOCIATE ONE. Sir Aston Amoeba and Dame Stella Frigidaire.

SEGIS. Oh.

(*a beat*)

Who are they?

ASSOCIATE TWO. Aston was on a leash and Stella turned a room into an ocean.

SEGIS. *(excited)* That woman…

(Suddenly, the light in the elevator floor indicator flickers and shorts.)

Huh. Someone must have blown the fuse.

ASSOCIATE ONE. The temp!

ASSOCIATE THREE. She's gone!

ASSOCIATE FOUR. She like, sabotaged us?

ASSOCIATE ONE. Oh snap!

ASSOCIATE TWO. What'll

ASSOCIATE THREE. we

ASSOCIATE FOUR. like do?

(SEGIS thinks a moment. He unplugs the phone and removes the cord. He moves to the back wall and strings the cord up in a rectangle shape from the floor, forming a crooked door.)

(SEGIS then notices something glowing down the front of his pants.)

Ha!!!!

(He feels around. He reaches in and retrieves a glowing stapler from his underwear. He presses it into the wall on the right-hand side, horizontally. It stays put. He then pulls down on the stapler, turning it like a doorknob. The "door" opens. A set of stairs is revealed.)

THE ASSOCIATES. Whoa.

(SEGIS removes the stapler from the door and holds it like a torch or a flashlight to light the steps.)

SEGIS. Seventy-seven floors to go. Kick it.

(They exit into the stairs. Lights out on the basement.)

*(The main office. Decorations for a retirement party; balloons, signs [GOOD LUCK BILL!], a swank spread of sumptuous foodstuffs. Perhaps a disco ball twirls,. Maybe a slideshow of **BILL BASIL** through the years is being set up on a screen somewhere. The receptionist desk has been turned into a bar/DJ booth.)*

(**ROSE** *storms in. She is wearing a fierce party dress with the price tag still attached. Her hair and nails and makeup are done up and she looks anything but cheap. She clutches the padded mailer in one hand and Aston's cellphone in the other.*)

(**ROSE** *grabs a cup and downs several glasses of punch in quick angry determined succession.*)

ROSE. Okay okay okay.

Got the fingernails got the face got the bling.

Shoes hair lips

Bing-bang-boom.

I show up with GAME, buddy.

A white hot ball of fierce.

Can't look at me can you?

Too hot, that's right.

She may jingle in your pocket

But I burn right through to your skin

Scorch your thigh hairs

I am THAT SICK.

(*She brandishes the phone and the package. Is about to dial. Falters. Drinks. Psyches herself up again.*)

Ha.

You think I can't bring it?

Oh I will BAAAH-RING it, Mr. Martin.

I will bring it CRAZY HIDEOUS.

Seven tiny numbers

Seven tiny numbers will LIQUEFY you.

All I have to do

is press 'em.

(**STELLA** *enters, carrying a gown in a bag. She is crying a little. She does not see* **ROSE.**)

ROSE. (*shocked*) Stella?

STELLA. (*quickly snapping out of it*) Oh, my. My dress. It's clean. I cry at clean things. You were supposed to pick this up from storage a week and a half ago.

ROSE. I got sick. Food poisoning.

STELLA. Not too poisoned to hit up Neiman Marcus I see.

(**STELLA** *grabs the price tag and reads it.*)

You can't afford this. Is it stolen?

ROSE. Borrowed, I was going to return it to the store after the party.

(**STELLA** *rips the price tag off.*)

Wait!

STELLA. It's on me.

ROSE. What? I couldn't!

STELLA. If *you* don't look good, *I* don't look good.

(*softer*)

Besides. I've been where you are. It's no picnic.

ROSE. Thanks Stella.

(*small beat*)

STELLA. (*hard again*) I don't like women. The way they laugh, the way they smell. The way they make themselves small. Flatten their little bodies and roll themselves out on the floor like a hallway runner, only to ask later, "Where did these footprints come from?"

And. I don't like men who act or laugh or smell like women. My advice? Never sleep with a man who owns more skin products than you.

(**STELLA** *exits. She returns a split second later.*)

The younger Mr. Basil wasn't here, was he?

ROSE. No.

STELLA. (*more to herself*) Thought I felt something…

(*She exits.*)

(*Beat.* **ROSE** *contemplates the package again. She contemplates the phone again. She looks after* **STELLA**.)

ROSE. *(quietly)* Seven tiny numbers...seven tiny numbers...

(She dials seven tiny numbers.)

Hello, Associated Press? Hi. My name is Anonymous. A-N-O – okay. I would like to inform you of a rather shocking scandal about to break over at BASIL ENTERPRISES...Yes. Bill Basil's retirement party.... It involves the current C.O.O., Mister Aston Martin...

(She downs a full glass of punch and pours herself another.)

(FRED CLOTALDO *enters, dressed in a lovely suit.* **ROSE** *jumps, startled.)*

FRED CLOTALDO. You're here?

ROSE. I work here.

FRED CLOTALDO. I haven't seen you in weeks.

ROSE. So?

(an awkward beat)

FRED CLOTALDO. *(genuine)* I'm sorry about our ah, our / less than decorous

ROSE. Die in a snowbank.

FRED CLOTALDO. Yes, that.

ROSE. Whatever.

(a beat)

My mother can be a bitch sometimes, so.

FRED CLOTALDO. All right.

(beat)

Um. Listen /

(CLAIRE *rushes in, hysterical.)*

CLAIRE. BOSS! BOSS!

FRED CLOTALDO. Claire! / What...

CLAIRE. Something DREADFUL has happened!

FRED CLOTALDO. Calm down...Breathe...

CLAIRE. The associates are in revolt!

FRED CLOTALDO. What?

CLAIRE. And Mr. Basil Junior is leading the charge! We need to tell Mr. Basil Senior!

FRED CLOTALDO. Why don't you go look for him?

CLAIRE. Me?

FRED CLOTALDO. Call every golf course, every yacht club, every aviation school in a fifteen mile radius. Check the steam rooms of the local health clubs, the cigar lounges of the tobacco purveyors, the scotch dens of the whisky importers. Call the high-end tailors. Call the mayor's office, the governor's mansion, the commissioner's lair. Call the zoo. He likes to pet the sheep sometimes.

CLAIRE. I won't let you down!

(to **ROSE***)*

Nice dress...

(She disappears. **FRED CLOTALDO** *turns to* **ROSE***.)*

FRED CLOTALDO. Listen, you should...

ROSE. Have another? Don't mind if I do.

(She knocks back her punch.)

FRED CLOTALDO. Okay we should definitely address your drinking at some point but right now I need you to leave this building. It could get very dangerous / here and I'm not

ROSE. Can't. Sorry. Got BUSINESS.

(Suddenly, **SEGIS** *and the* **ASSOCIATES** *crash through the ceiling and into the party.)*

FRED CLOTALDO. Good lord –

SEGIS. HA! ALL RIGHT PEOPLE, PREPARE TO...where is everyone?

FRED CLOTALDO. The accountants are stuck in HR under mountains of paperwork. You fired them two weeks ago and legally they need to be on payroll before we can feed them.

ASSOCIATE THREE. Dudes, how can we wage a take-over when there's no one to overtake?

SEGIS. We'll face our enemies in due time. For now, LET'S KARAOKE!!

(**SEGIS** *grabs the karaoke mic. and begins a soaring rendition of "Goodbye Yellow Brick Road,"* though he doesn't know all the words so he makes some of them up.*)

(*The* **ASSOCIATES** *form a sorry conga line and conga listlessly to* **SEGIS***'s song.*)

ROSE. *(re: listless conga line)* I've never seen them so motivated.

(**FRED** *is about to exit.* **ROSE** *and* **FRED** *talk over* **SEGIS***'s song.*)

Where are you going?

FRED CLOTALDO. I have loyalties…

ROSE. To whom?

FRED CLOTALDO. To the company, to Bill Basil/

ROSE. I'M YOUR FLESH AND EFFING BLOOD!!

(*He hands her the ornate pen from earlier.*)

FRED CLOTALDO. Take this. You'll need it.

(**FRED** *exits.*)

ROSE. He abandoned me! AGAIN!! I'm too sober for this….

(*An* **ASSOCIATE** *congas by and hands her a drink. She downs it and hands the empty glass to another* **ASSOCIATE** *on the conga line.*)

DOES ANYONE HAVE ANY GUM? I'm losing my nerve. I can't do this alone and NO ONE WILL HELP ME!

(**SEGIS** *spots* **ROSE.**)

SEGIS. *(pointing)* Ha!

ROSE. *(jumps)* Ah!

---

* Please see Music Use Note on Page 3.

SEGIS. You!

ROSE. Who!

SEGIS. YOU who.

ROSE. What?

SEGIS. Were there.

ROSE. Where?

SEGIS. Before.

ROSE. When?

SEGIS. Before!

ROSE. Before what?

SEGIS. Before, earlier! After later!

ROSE. ALCOHOL. NOW.

SEGIS. *After* an alarm went off. *Before* they told me it was a dream.

ROSE. How did you make them conga?

SEGIS. They're in a conga of their own volition.

ROSE. You inspired it. I saw.

SEGIS. What happened to me, Rose?

ROSE. Inspire them to turn on their webcams. For their vlogs. They all have vlogs.

SEGIS. What happened to me, Rose?

ROSE. Someone stuck you with a big needle and you passed out.

SEGIS. Who?

ROSE. My dad. Fred Clotaldo.

SEGIS. Your DAD??

ROSE. He had orders.

SEGIS. From whom?

ROSE. *(exasperated) Your* dad.

> (**SEGIS** *grabs his heart in pain.*)

Yeah. When fathers act like jerks it hurts. Now I told you what you wanted, will you help me?

> (**ASTON** *enters in a swanky suit. He is shocked to see* **SEGIS.**)

ASTON. *(to* **SEGIS***)* What are you doing here?

ROSE. He's cleaning up your mess.

ASTON. *(totally off guard)* Rose!

SEGIS. *(on the mic)* Ladies and Gentlemen, it's time for the "raffle."

ASTON. What the hell is going on?

> (**SEGIS** *gestures to a gift basket.*)

SEGIS. *(on the mic)* A wicker basket filled with New York-style bagel chips, pasteurized cheese spread, Scottish short-bread cookies, a jar of Cajun mustard, some caramel popcorn, decaf hazelnut coffee packets, and a tiny little pot of bilberry jam.

> (**ROSE** *hands* **ASTON** *the padded mailer from earlier.*)

ASTON. What's this?

ROSE. Open it.

> (**ASTON** *opens it carefully. Inside is a manila envelope.*)

SEGIS. Associates, turn on your web-cams.

> (*The* **ASSOCIATES** *rush to their computers and turn on their webcams.* **ASTON**'s *image is now projected on a screen somewhere in the room, visible to all. He is unaware.*)

> (*A news helicopter appears outside.*)

ASTON. What…

ROSE. Found it cleaning my apartment last month…

ASTON. *(reading)* "Affidavit of application for marriage license…" You're married!!?? Who are you married to?

ROSE. *("duh")* Keep reading.

ASTON. *(utter shock)* ME????!!!

(in recognition) Vegas.

> (*All the phones and cellphones and blackberries in the room begin to ring. The* **ASSOCIATES** *tend to them frantically, chattering.*)

ASSOCIATE ONE. Our shareholders, "what's going on – ?"

ASSOCIATE TWO. The AP, "who's in charge – ?"

ASSOCIATE THREE. Ferris Investments, "are we for sale – ?"

ASSOCIATE FOUR. Terra Sushi, "send the edamame back – ?"

   (**SEGIS** *picks up a basket of raffle tickets and grabs one.*)

SEGIS. *(on the mic)* Get out your "tickets"…

   (*Suddenly,* **BILL BASIL** *arrives, in his Armani suit and tie. He is surrounded by his* **ACCOUNTANTS**, *with* **FRED CLOTALDO** *not far behind.*)

   (*They are projected on the screen.*)

SEGIS. *(weighted)* Hello, dad.

BILL BASIL. Hello, son.

SEGIS. Sorry we drank all your retirement punch.

BILL BASIL. Perfectly fine, considering I'm no longer retiring.

SEGIS. My employees here are celebrating your departure…

BILL BASIL. You can't possibly expect me to hand over my life's work and watch you destroy it.

SEGIS. You set me up for failure.

BILL BASIL. And fail you did. Miserably. Now if you don't mind, this function is reserved for mid-to-upper level employees. Please withdraw immediately.

   (**BILL BASIL** *gestures to the* **ACCOUNTANTS**. *They move in threateningly.*)

SEGIS. I'll die before I go back to customer service…

   (**STELLA** *rushes in wearing an astonishing ballgown.*)

STELLA. You won't have to. I'll teach you how to run this business. No one knows it like me. Not even you, Bill.

   (*to* **ASTON**)

   I caught everything. Online. At least she's no bimbo. I hope you two have a miraculous life together.

   (**SEGIS** *grabs the mic.*)

SEGIS. *(waving the raffle ticket)* Friends! The winning combination!

(The **ASSOCIATES** *arm themselves and move to protect* **SEGIS.** **SEGIS** *reads from the ticket.)*

M. U. T. I. N. Y.

(small beat)

BILL BASIL. Very well.

(Music kicks in.)

(An incredibly acrobatic fight breaks out between the **ASSOCIATES** *and the* **ACCOUNTANTS,** *with men and women tumbling about the office machinery, wounding each other with paper-cuts, scissor-gashes, packing-tape-bindings, etc. It goes on forever. It seems they are physically fighting over who gets to control the spin. It's old media vs. new media. Old media is trying to see in [post-it notes block view through window, etc.] and phone in, but underground self-publishing tools actively deliver the dominant message of* **SEGIS** *taking over (webcams, twittering, texting, etc).)*

(Amid the fighting, **STELLA** *grabs the marriage license and turns one of the webcams toward herself.)*

(All talk and fight simultaneously.)

ASTON. Stella –

STELLA. *(to the cameras)* My fiancé…a would-be bigamist! Rather than subject this company to more opprobrium, I am going to ask that Aston Martin resign.

ASTON. Wait a second…

ROSE. HIS REAL NAME IS REGINALD!!

ASTON. Blast you!

*(***ASTON** *lunges for* **ROSE.** *She unsheathes the ornate pen from earlier, but doesn't know how to use it.)*

ROSE. Shit! How does this work?! Dad!!

FRED CLOTALDO. In this order –

ASTON. "DAD???"

FRED CLOTALDO. – stroke the diamond fretwork, turn the gold band, press the platinum shirt-clip!!

(*She does. The pen becomes a fantastic weapon.*)

ROSE. WHOA! Thank you!

FRED CLOTALDO. Any time!

(*Fighting continues.*)

(*Suddenly,* **CLAIRE** *bursts in, out of breath, wearing an atrocious outfit that screams "LOOK AT ME!!" She runs straight to* **FRED CLOTALDO**, *not seeing* **BILL BASIL** *at first.*)

(*No one stops fighting.*)

CLAIRE. I checked every spot you mentioned for Mr. Basil, boss...I also checked the hospitals, the homeless people, the porn shops.... NO ONE has seen him. And THEN I had to get an outfit for the *gala*, which was a whole nother ordeal because I've never been to a *gala* before and I didn't know the dress code –

(**CLAIRE** *finally notices* **BILL BASIL**.)

You're HERE! How long have you, why didn't anyone...

(*slow recognization*)

Oh. I get it. It was on purpose. You were TRYING to keep me away.

FRED CLOTALDO. It was for your own pro/tection.

CLAIRE. (*still small*) After all the work I did for you? I tried so hard. I never asked for anything from anyone. All I wanted was a thank you...

(*to* **ROSE**)

"THANK YOU CLAIRE for cleaning my dishes when I was too hungover to do it myself..."

(*to the* **ASSOCIATES**)

"THANK YOU CLAIRE for being wildly entertaining when we nearly expired from boredom..."

(*to* **BILL**, **ASTON**, **STELLA**)

CLAIRE. *(cont.)* "THANK YOU CLAIRE for not leaking my horrible lies to anyone who would listen..."

(to **SEGIS***)*

"THANK YOU CLAIRE FOR POURING FIVE-HUNDRED AND TWENTY-SEVEN SELTZERS THAT I NEVER EVEN DRANK!!"

*(***CLAIRE*** separates herself from the gang and gets into oratorical mode.)*

You can't treat employees like they're invisible and expect them to stay loyal! You need to THANK your people.

*(***CLAIRE*** does a bizarre dance, going from employee to employee screaming "THANK YOU!" at each one, until...)*

BILL BASIL. You're fired.

(The fighting stops a moment.)

CLAIRE. *(heartbroken)* I'm, I'm fired?? Oh. Okay. Sorry everyone. Bye.

*(***CLAIRE*** grabs a spring roll, takes a small sad crunchy bite, and skulks off.)*

*(***SEGIS*** signals to the* **ASSOCIATES***. The* **ASSOCIATES** *shed their lame party outfits. They are wearing truly weird things beneath, things that somehow express their inner selves.)*

(A beat, then the fracas turns freaky, and the office becomes a circus. TRULY SURREAL SHIT happens in slow motion. Throughout it all the **ASSOCIATES** *remain absurdly bored and the* **ACCOUNTANTS** *remain absurdly austere. It is weird.)*

(But magical. AND. It is clear that **STELLA** *and* **SEGIS** *are making this magic.)*

*(***STELLA*** fights* **FRED CLOTALDO***, and wins.)*

(The **ASSOCIATES** *beat the* **ACCOUNTANTS***.)*

*(***ROSE*** beats* **ASTON***. He submits.)*

*(**SEGIS** and **BILL BASIL** are facing off.)*

*(Someone in the room turns on a live broadcast. A **TV CAMERAMAN** appears in the room. The live feed is projected.)*

BROADCAST. Breaking story over at Basil Enterprises…In a shocking turn of events, Bill Basil's son is defeating his father for control of the Basil empire. It appears that office supplies and new media are the weapons of choice, and –

*(**BILL BASIL**'s legs buckle and he drops to his knees.)*

SEGIS. Dad…

BILL BASIL. Do it! I've seen the tyrant in you.

SEGIS. I'm, I'm not like you….

BILL BASIL. All those articles you saved tell me something different. I know it in your core.

You're a Basil.

*(A beat. The **ASSOCIATES** and **ACCOUNTANTS** lean in, breathless.)*

BILL BASIL. The world is watching, son.

SEGIS. I…

BILL BASIL. Do it. CRUSH ME.

*(**SEGIS** roars and grabs something as if he is going to beat his father to death with it.)*

*(A beat. Slowly, **SEGIS** backs off. He turns the cameras onto himself.)*

SEGIS. [insert proper date] "June __, 20__. In a move that seems contrary to BASIL ENTERPRISES' former business practices, incoming President Segis Basil spearheaded the company's first 'friendly takeover…'"

*(He glances at **STELLA** and smiles.)*

"…with the support of current C.E.O., Stella Strong."

*(**STELLA** smiles back.)*

(SEGIS holds out his hand to help his father up, who is still shaking violently.)

(a beat)

(BILL BASIL takes his hand.)

(The ASSOCIATES cheer boredly. They go back to their desks and work while the ACCOUNTANTS attempt to party, badly.)

(Meanwhile, ROSE and ASTON realize they are clutching each other.)

ASTON. *(impressed)* You infiltrated a multi-billion dollar company. You turned the press against me. You beat me at my own game.

ROSE. It was never your game in the first place, Reggie.

ASTON. You're right. I'm a gecko.

ROSE. You are.

ASTON. I'm unemployed now

ROSE. I know.

ASTON. I want to be a farmer.

ROSE. You don't know how to farm.

ASTON. I can learn.

ROSE. *(joke)* You don't know how to learn.

ASTON. I can dig.

ROSE. You'll be dirt poor.

ASTON. *We'll* be dirt poor.

> *(ROSE smiles.)*
>
> *(They engage in a slow-motion-climbing love-dance, saying things very softly to each other, trance-like. We don't necessarily have to hear their words at all.)*

ROSE. *(very very softly, over BILL and SEGIS)* Sonnet

ASTON. Kaleidoscope

ROSE. Glitter

ASTON. Refrain

ROSE. Envelope

ASTON. Follicle

ROSE. Twilight

ASTON. Epigram

ROSE. Halo

ASTON. Vermillion

ROSE. Galaxy

ASTON. Subsequent

ROSE. Amber

ASTON. Azalea

ROSE. Satchel

ASTON. Rose

ROSE. Amulet

ASTON. Rose

ROSE. Hologram

ASTON. Rose

ROSE. Memory

ASTON. Rose

ROSE. Fever

ASTON. Rose

ROSE. Trachea

ASTON. Rose

ROSE. Interval

ASTON. Rose

ROSE. Caramel

ASTON. Rose

ROSE. Fingertip

ASTON. Rose

ROSE. Temple

ASTON. Rose

ROSE. Navel

ASTON. Rose

ROSE. Forehead

ASTON. Rose

ROSE. Lips

ASTON. Rose

ROSE. Lover

ASTON. Rose

ROSE. Yes

ASTON. Rose

ROSE. Yes

ASTON. Rose

ROSE. Yes

> *(They continue to repeat the last two words as long as it takes for* **BILL BASIL** *and* **SEGIS** *to finish.)*

SEGIS. Have you been to the doctor about / your hands

BILL BASIL. Don't care about this piece of refuse before you. Care about what he's built. This is his empire. This is his dream.

> *(a beat)*

SEGIS. *Was.*

It's my dream now.

> *(***SEGIS*** *retrieves the wicker basket filled with goodies and hands it to his father.)*

Happy Retirement.

> *(With dignity, and still wracked with tremors,* **BILL BASIL** *accepts the basket. He turns to* **FRED CLOTALDO**.*)*

BILL BASIL. Fred? Are you coming?

> *(***FRED*** *glances over at his daughter.)*

FRED CLOTALDO.*(quietly)* No, Bill.

> *(A beat.* **BILL BASIL** *exits.)*

> *(***ASTON*** *and* **ROSE** *stop climbing and lock into an embrace.)*

> *(***SEGIS*** *gathers himself.)*

SEGIS. Fred. I'd like a meeting first thing tomorrow morning. Major debriefing. I want the accountants present, all of them, with paperwork from the last few quarters, and I'll need a huge pot of coffee and some scones for everyone…wait a second. What exactly is your job?

FRED CLOTALDO. I'm the office manager.

SEGIS. Oh. Would you like to be Vice President in charge of operations?

FRED CLOTALDO. No.

SEGIS. Really? Are you sure?

FRED CLOTALDO. Positive. But I wouldn't mind a raise…it's been a while.

SEGIS. I'll tell payroll.

FRED CLOTALDO. Thank you.

(beat)

SEGIS. *(with some difficulty and awkwardness, but genuine)* No. Thank YOU.

*(**FRED CLOTALDO** smiles kindly, a smile of forgiveness.)*

FRED CLOTALDO. You're welcome.

SEGIS. And get that nutty girl back. I need a PA.

FRED CLOTALDO. Right away.

*(**FRED CLOTALDO** exits.)*

SEGIS. Associates?

THE ASSOCIATES. Yeah?

SEGIS. Why are you working? This is a party.

ASSOCIATE THREE. We grew weary of the revelry.

ASSOCIATE TWO. We have abject lethargy.

ASSOCIATE FOUR. And like, poor nutrition?

SEGIS. Well, make sure you clock in your overtime.

ASSOCIATE TWO. *(re: his computer screen)* Our stocks are climbing!

ASSOCIATE FOUR. Our website's traffic has like, quadrupled?

ASSOCIATE THREE. This coffee is DELICIOUS!

ASSOCIATE ONE. I DIG MY JOB, SUCKAS!

SEGIS. Stella?

STELLA. Yes?

SEGIS. What do we do now?

STELLA. You mean what do YOU do now. You need to personally call every one of our investors and apologize profusely for a) the profoundly abysmal performance of this company over the past few months and b) the shit-storm of publicity we just received.

(re: the webcams)

Turn those off.

(They do. STELLA kisses SEGIS forcefully.)

Next. You buy yourself a blackberry, an iPhone, and a beeper. Use one as a stock ticker, one as a communication device, and one to buzz me when you need a –

(SEGIS kisses STELLA forcefully. She melts a little.)

– consultation.

(Something magical happens. The room turns into an ocean.)

(thrilled) It's happening again…

SEGIS. What do you think of BASIL AND STRONG ENTERPRISES?

STELLA. Not as good as STRONG AND BASIL ENTERPRISES.

SEGIS. Merger of the decade.

(She has a genuine smile, the first we've ever seen. She holds him.)

I can do this. Can't I.

STELLA. You can.

SEGIS. I don't have to be him.

STELLA. You don't.

SEGIS. Is this my fever dream?

STELLA. What do you think?

SEGIS. I think...

I'm going to be a benevolent billionaire.

(**SEGIS** *looks around surveying his empire.*)

(*Somehow, the room transforms magically...*)

(*The fluorescent light continues to buzz, though the buzzing becomes music, much like the fizzing seltzers did earlier.*)

(*The* **ASSOCIATES** *typing at their computers slowly disappear – or else their typing becomes part of the music, and their movements become dreamlike.*)

(*Lights down.*)

End of Play

OTHER TITLES AVAILABLE FROM SAMUEL FRENCH

LASCIVIOUS SOMETHING

Sheila Callaghan

Drama / 1m, 3f / Single Set

On a secluded Greek island, an American ex-pat pursues his passions: winemaking and his breathtaking young wife. Then, on the eve of Reagan's inauguration, the first tasting of the new wine is interrupted by the unexpected arrival of August's former lover. Inspired by Greek tragedy, *Lascivious Something* combines evocative language with sympathetic yet deeply flawed characters straight out of Euripides.

"Definitely worth spending an undeniably tense evening with, right through an unexpected twist at the end."
– Associated Press

"Sheila Callaghan has created a great premise and fascinating characters, her writing intertwining wine and blood and sex as painful but necessary life forces."
– Back Stage

"Sometimes dreamlike, often shocking, *Lascivious Something* is at once both fraught and languorous, its most powerful moments found in the quietest revelations or silent stares. Go with an open mind and you are certain to find that your cup runneth over with ideas by the final bow."
– The Collective Magazine

"Callaghan, whose previous work might be described as post-feminist punk incursions into the poetic turf of early Sam Shepard, here employs a more linear narrative line to push her personal-is-political agenda."
– LA Weekly

"Blown Away...Honest, captivating from beginning to end. I can't recommend it enough"
– CBS News

OTHER TITLES AVAILABLE FROM SAMUEL FRENCH

ROADKILL CONFIDENTIAL

Sheila Callaghan

Thriller/Mystery / 3m, 2f

A noir-ish meditation on brutality

A possibly rogue g-man stalks a stalled-out artist with a suspicious affinity for accident victims. Traps are set, traps are sprung, and everyone gets caught. *Roadkill Confidential* attempts to tackle, with style, humor and high theatricality, mediated violence and the numbness it produces, and, whether in art or in global politics, the ends can justify the means.

OTHER TITLES AVAILABLE FROM SAMUEL FRENCH

CRAWL, FADE TO WHITE

Sheila Callaghan

Dramatic Comedy / 2m, 3f / Simple Set

A scream is heard throughout the stratosphere. It is the voice of the lamp. Louise is selling this expensive family heirloom to keep her daughter April in school and cease her more sordid "consultant" profession. April rushes home with lover in tow to halt the proceedings and save the lamp, but it has been intercepted by a quiet and bizarre middle-aged couple with a haunting secret.

Attempts to reclaim the lamp are made, as a misplaced father slowly fades to white in the background.

"…A gutsy writer with a gift for creating vivid images rooted in the emotional life of her characters."
– *The New York Times*

"…Troubled and precocious college dropout April is described to her mother, Louise, as 'stunningly brilliant' – a line that fits her creator, Sheila Callaghan. The odd characters populating *Crawl, Fade to White* frantically eat dirt and twist menacingly. Audiences trying to process this engagingly quirky new play might find themselves gaping 'like they're watching the cosmos disrobe.'"
– *Time Out New York*

OTHER TITLES AVAILABLE FROM SAMUEL FRENCH

WE ARE NOT THESE HANDS

Sheila Callaghan

Comedy / 1m, 2f / Simple Set

Ever since their school blew up, Moth and Belly have taken to stalking an illegal internet café in the hopes of one day being allowed in. They take particular interest in Leather, a skittish older man doing research in the café.

Leather is a self-proclaimed "freelance scholar" from a foreign land with a sketchy past and a sticky secret. Leather begins to fall head over heals in love with Moth... but what about Belly? This play explores the effects of rampant capitalism on a country that is ill-prepared for it.

"Bold and engaging, *We Are Not These Hands* is as fun as it is engaging...Rich in detail and full of humor and pathos."
– *Oakland Tribune*

"Swaggering eccentricity...Callaghan takes a lavish mud bath in a broken language...Ripe apocalyptic slang; at its best, it's racy and unrefined, the kind of stuff you might imagine kids in the back alleys of a decaying world might sling around."
– *The Washington Post*

"The gap between rich and poor yawns so wide it aches in Sheila Callaghan's *We Are Not These Hands*, but much of the ache is from laughter. *Hands* is a comically engaging, subversively penetrating look at the human cost of unbridled capitalism on both sides of the river...the anger of the play's social vision is partly concealed by its copious humor, emerging more forcefully after it's over...*Hands* bristles with bright, comic originality, particularly in depicting the limitations of its people."
– *San Francisco Chronicle*